Christmas 1993

For Jenny, with love
from Grandpa

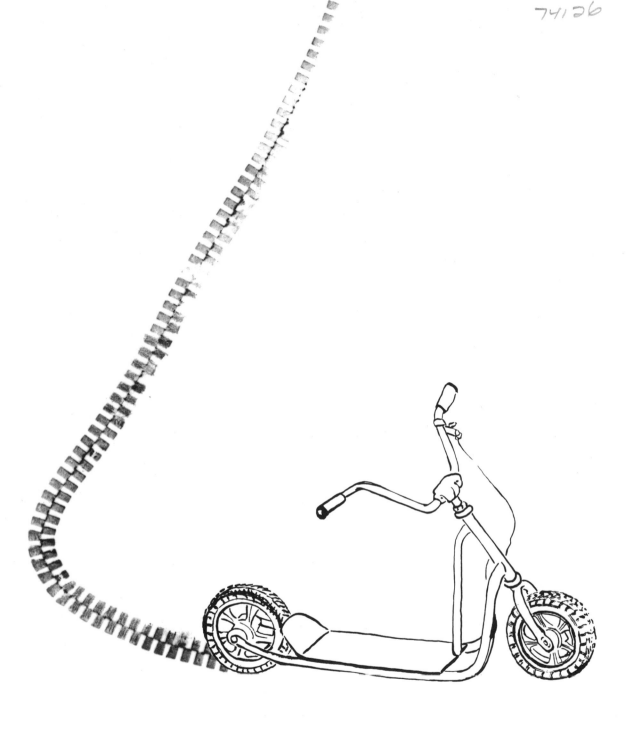

Vera B. Williams

SCOOTER

GREENWILLOW BOOKS, NEW YORK

Scooter owes some of its features and spirit to a book, The One of a Kind Class, made for me in 1986 by Class 3-305, P.S. 166, in Long Island City, New York. My thanks to that wonderful class and their teacher, wherever they may be now.

And special thanks to Sylvie Le Floc'h for her patient and expert help with putting the many parts of this book together.

Library of Congress
Cataloging-in-Publication Data

Williams, Vera B.
Scooter / by Vera B. Williams
    p.   cm.
Summary: A child's silver blue scooter
helps her adjust to her new home.
ISBN 0-688-09376-0 (trade)
ISBN 0-688-09377-9 (lib. bdg.)
[1. Scooters—Fiction.
2. Moving, Household—Fiction.
3. Divorce—Fiction. 4. Friendship—Fiction.
5. Mothers and daughters—Fiction.]
I. Title.   PZ7.W6685Sc   1993
[Fic]—dc20   90-38489   CIP   AC

TO
NEW YORK CITY
WHERE I GREW UP
AND TO MY SISTER
OMI (NAOMI) WITH WHOM
I SHARED THAT SPECIAL TIME

CONTENTS

Scooter
Can't you
Open the door?
Open that front door!
Take
Elana out....
Ride and ride

Now I LOVE living here. I like the address. You take the one from the five so you get the four . . . 514 Melon Hill Avenue, Apartment 8E. <u>E</u> is my first initial. The highest up I ever lived before was on the third floor when we stayed with my cousins.

514 Melon Hill Avenue is a great big building. And it's together with four other big buildings. They call them the Melon Hill Houses. They are at the top of Melon Hill. And they have water towers and a brick wall around the roofs that makes them look like castles.

I was a real Melon Hill House kid from day one! But my mom says not so, and that I stood at our window for days just staring out. Well, of course, I <u>was</u> amazed. From that window I could see buildings spread out right to the edge of the river and then bridges and more buildings across the river. When the lights went on for nighttime I couldn't believe there could be so many lights in so many houses on so many streets and us not know anyone in any of those houses. I could see the big school where I'm going to go after the summer. I didn't know a single person in that school. And all our clothes and stuff were in boxes.

My scooter was the very last thing we packed onto the trailer when we moved out from over the garage at Grandma and Grandpa's house. After we drove a thousand miles my scooter was the first thing I brought up in the elevator with my mom to our new apartment here on the eighth floor of 514 Melon Hill Avenue.

Our one-room apartment was empty. It smelled of new paint. I put my scooter right by the window. Whenever I wasn't helping get our stuff unpacked and put away I stood on my scooter and looked out the window.

Almost every single hour, my mom would ask me why I didn't go out and play.

My mom: "When are you going to stop moping and go out and play?"

Me: "<u>Who</u> am I going to play with?"

2

My mom: "I *see* lots of kids down there. All colors and sizes. They look great to me."

Me: "But I don't <u>know</u> any of those kids. . . ."

My mom: "Well, you never will if you don't go out. Kids won't come to our door just seeking out the famous and beautiful Elana Rose Rosen."

Me: "I didn't say they would."

My mom: "Elana, please! Did I say <u>you</u> said it? And don't start to cry! I have too much to do to get involved in scenes with you. I have to get us settled. Find a job. Get ready for my courses."

Me: "Just leave me here alone then."

My mom: "But it breaks my heart to see you standing on that scooter, moping."

Me: "I'm not moping."

Finally my mom came right up behind me and put her hands on the handlebars and pushed me and the scooter out our front door and down the hall and into the elevator and out the elevator and through the lobby. Then she gave me a big push that sent me out the front doors where the intercom is and into the courtyard.

"There's no kids out here," I called to her.

"You've got your scooter," she answered. She was already going through the door.

"Come down in a little while," I yelled after her.

"See you at supper time," she said, waving.

EEK!
MAJOR SMASH-UP!
EEEEK!
RUSH!
GRAB CAB!
EEEEEK!
NO TIME TO THINK!
CAN ONLY
YELL "HOSPITAL QUICK!"

I PUSHED ON into the courtyard. It was bright and blurry. Sun bounced off the chrome of my scooter.

Outside our building, 514, and between the other Melon Hill buildings, there's a long sidewalk. It's great to ride on. The very first day my mom brought me here, when the trailer was being unloaded, I watched the other kids riding bikes there. There's a really smooth cement ramp. It has wide, flat steps that make a drop just right to jump the scooter.

I was practicing jumping my scooter. I could already even it up fast on the straightaway so there was no wobble. Then I started practicing my double heel click. That's a very special trick I invented. You have to have good balance to try it. And you have to have lots of room, so don't try it on a short runway. Get going fast. Then lean with all your might on the handlebars. Let your legs go way up in back and knock them together fast as you can. Then knock them together again. Simple? It's truly a beautiful trick. I've since even learned to do a triple heel click. But I bet nobody can do a quadruple.

Of course, you do have to have a good scooter. Mine has great balance on account of it has such tremendous wheels. It's beautiful, too. The wheels have a wide silver line all around and a skinny blue stripe like a ribbon around the silver.

Mostly then I was practicing jumps. They were spectacular. After supper my mom came down to watch. It stayed light late then. High up between the buildings you could see a piece of sky turning a special blue. I got my mother to sit so she could see me driving right toward her.

I got a quick start, and I was going fast. Then suddenly there was a big loose thing like a whole piece of sidewalk

5

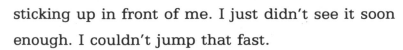

sticking up in front of me. I just didn't see it soon
enough. I couldn't jump that fast.

I landed smash on my face. I think my mom screamed. I
think she shook me. She grabbed me and ran out to the street
with me. Someone helped us get one of those yellow taxis and
told the driver the name of the hospital to take me to.

In the cab I held on to my mother. I was scared of all
the blood. I was excited, too. I hoped the taxi would go
fast like an ambulance. I wished it had a siren.

The taxi bounced a lot. My mother held her arm tight
around me. She talked and cried. She said at least I didn't
lose any of my beautiful teeth. She said I was too wild for my
own good. She said she was definitely sending the scooter
back to Grandma and Grandpa. That made me cry. I said I
would go with it if she sent it back. She said I mustn't cry, it
made my chin bleed more. She held more tissues to my chin.

The taxi driver started to talk. He told us how he cut
his head real bad falling out of a tree when he was a kid.
He said to look at the scar on the back of his head. That
man was so kind he wouldn't even let my mom pay. He
ran into the emergency room with us to show us the way.

The nurse looked at my head and my chin and said the
doctor would take care of me soon. Then I had to wait
and wait. The arrow with the word EMERGENCY was
made of red, red light that kept moving up the arrow. It

6

looked the way the blood pounding in my head felt. The bottom part of my face was getting stiff and couldn't feel.

There was a man with a bandage on his foot bigger than a basketball, even. My mom said not to stare. You see scary things in the hospital. It smells weird, too.

At last the doctor could sew up my cuts. It hurt, and I felt like I was going to be sick. I held so tight to my mother's hand that her hand got numb. My mother told the doctor I wouldn't have had this accident if I wasn't always such a wild kid on my scooter. She told the doctor I was so wild she didn't know what to do with me.

The doctor told my mother not to worry. It wasn't really such a bad accident for a stunt rider. She said I mustn't fall on my head again, though. She bandaged my chin extra thick. When she showed me my face in the mirror, the bandage looked tremendous. I loved the doctor.

I wanted to ride home in a taxi. I liked that taxi driver. My mom said we'd never get the same taxi again. And the bus came right then. I was so sleepy riding home in the bus that the red and green and yellow lights swam together. People's heads swam together. I can't even remember how I got into my bed. I still ask my mother, "But how did I get all the way up in the elevator and undressed and everything, and I didn't even know?"

Way later I woke up. It was in the middle of the middle

of the night. I couldn't see. I couldn't tell . . . was I in my grandpa and grandma's house? Was I in our old house with my father before he moved away? Were we still staying at my cousin Nanette's apartment, so full of my cousins' beds you could hardly walk? But on my cousins' street the streetcar went by all night long. How come I couldn't hear the streetcar? Why was there a big lumpy thing on my chin and on my head? And where was my scooter? <u>Where was my scooter?</u>

My mother says she just flew to me when she heard me yelling for my scooter.

She switched on the lights. On the wall between the windows, the funny little light made to look like a candle came on. There was my scooter right in the place I had made for it by the window. I stood on it and looked way down into the streets below. It was raining and the streets were black and wet. I thought I could see the bump that had tripped up my scooter.

"How did my scooter get back up here?" I asked my mother. She told me I was pretty lucky for such a reckless kid. One of our new neighbors, a little boy, Petey, had picked it up and set it by our door. There was just some mud on the wheels and stuff.

"What did he say?" I asked.

"Nothing," my mom said. "He just brought it and stood

there . . . wouldn't say a word. Then he went away."

My mom made us cocoa. I had to drink it in little sips. I tried a cookie, but the bandage made it hard to chew. We sat wrapped up in blankets in the kitchen. Our bathrobes seemed to have disappeared when we moved. My mom says if we have to keep moving finally everything will get lost. Boxes from our dishes were still around us. You never saw so many boxes as when you move. My mom just couldn't wait till she got enough time to get rid of all the boxes. But I liked it. It felt as if we were camping.

Our big blue pot with speckles and our frying pan and our toaster were sitting around the legs of my chair. I told my mom that the big blue pot was asking the frying pan and the toaster how they liked their new kitchen.

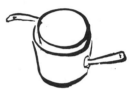

My mom said she thought the big blue pot was saying how glad it was that I was okay, and the toaster was saying how it hoped I would be able to eat toast real soon. I laughed, but that hurt my chin, too. Then I took my cocoa to my bed.

But I didn't even get back in my bed. I found a rag so I could clean every bit of mud off my scooter. I looked through the boxes and found the one marked FIX. I got the little squirt can of oil out. I oiled the wheels. Then I polished and I polished the silver stripe with the blue stripe like a ribbon around it till I made those stripes so bright you could even see them in the dark.

9

3

FRIENDS
REALLY ARE
IMPORTANT,
ESPECIALLY
NICE FRIENDS.
DIFFICULT FRIENDS
SOMETIMES ARE GREAT TOO.

THE DAY AFTER the day after my accident I had to wait in the elevator a long time on seven. A lady was holding the door for her friend, who had run back to her apartment to unplug her iron even though everybody thought it wasn't fair to hold the elevator that long. I was telling Cecelia from right next door about my ride to the hospital. Then this kid ran into the elevator, saw it wasn't going anywhere and ran out, ducked back in, and pulled me out down the hall with him.

"You know me, I'm Jimmy Beck right under you in 7E. Listen, I'll show you how we get down fast in this building." He pushed open the heavy door to the fire stairs.

"I guess you know everything," I said, to be sarcastic. It's the meanest way I know to be, since I can't stand when people make sarcastic remarks to me. But it didn't bother him. He was leaping the steps from the seventh floor to the sixth in bunches. When I caught up with him on the landing, he was writing hard into the skin of his arm with a ballpoint: J.B. KNOWS EVERYTHING.

"Jimmy Beck knows everything," he sang, running down the stairs to five. I love to run and jump down stairs fast, too, and I wanted to see this back part of our building and where we'd come out. Only I couldn't run now. It made my head hurt. So Jimmy got to all the landings first. He jumped the last half of each flight and ran back up so he wouldn't ever have to stop talking.

From the fifth to the fourth, he told me Eduard with the skateboard lived in 4K and the scooter tricks he saw me doing were almost as good as Eduard's skateboard stuff. For a girl, that is, he added.

From the fourth to the third, he explained that he didn't get a skateboard because he got a fifteen-speed

11

instead, and did I know a kid named Vinh on the third floor?

From the third to the second, he told me he knew day before yesterday I was going to wreck up on that piece of broken pavement, and he had yelled at me to watch out, but I was too stuck-up to listen.

On the second, he stood still (sort of) to tell me he had once had an accident standing on a swing going over the top, and blood ran out his nose and his mouth and his ears and his eyes just like the Mississippi. Running again, he pointed down the hall and said a dumb little kid named Petey lived there. He made a sign with his finger that Petey was crazy.

On the first floor, he said Adrienne lived down the hall and her parents owned the variety store only they charged way too much for everything.

We finally pushed open the fire door to the outside. "C'mon," Jimmy called, racing for the courtyard. But I had had enough of Jimmy Beck, so I took my time. I wanted to explore every bit of Melon Hill Houses. There were two playgrounds and tables for games, I knew, but I had the feeling there was lots more to find than I had noticed right off.

I met a lot of kids that day and the next. And it was partly thanks to Jimmy Beck's big mouth, I have to admit.

Kids had heard about my accident, about lots of blood
(<u>much</u> more than there was) and about a scooter that had
huge silver and blue wheels and maybe you could get
rides on.

I'm not at all sure Jimmy Beck can be what I call a
friend. But Vinh or Eduard or Adrienne will be. All three
of us might do a lot of things together. They're all in the
same class in the school where I'll be going. I'll be in
their class, too, after the summer when we start school.

Siobhan and Beryl are in other classes. Beryl wears
lipstick already, and she likes to act sexy. And Adrienne
from the first floor, her mother is going to have a baby
real soon. Eduard's like me with my scooter. Only he's
much more of a single-minded person than I am about
wheels. He <u>never</u> goes out without his skateboard. He
even rides it in the halls. We're not allowed to ride in the
halls. But you should see how he can come right up to
the elevator door, then stop in one little inch!

Then there's Petey. I've heard the kids say things about
Petey. He's the little kid who brought home my scooter
after my accident. I haven't met him yet, but I know he
lives in my building and I know where. I bet it won't be
long, either, till I know every kid in this building.
But I am especially curious about Petey.

4

Look
Up, look down, look all around
Can't ever
Know for sure
Your lucky day!

A FEW DAYS AFTER my accident Adrienne rang our bell.
She wanted to see the bandage on my head. She was
never even in an apartment on the eighth floor before.
She said she liked standing up on the scooter and looking
out the window.

"I'd be so scared to live here, Lanny," she said.
"You're almost to the roof." She didn't really like it. She's
used to the first floor. Only she got excited when she
found Thieu's Variety Store. That's her parents' store.
Then she saw our school. "You can see pretty much from
up here," she said.

She asked me where I slept, so I showed her my couch.
Anyone can tell it's mine because mine is on my side of
our big room right by my scooter. It has the cover with
the rosy flowers. My mom's has the cover with brown and
blue flowers, and the rug is in between. And mine has
my old bear and my lion on it. I wanted my own room so
bad, but my mom said it would be quite awhile before
she could afford that. When I suggested she ask my
father for money for more rent, she said, like she usually
does, "Put that out of your mind, honey!" (But I never
really do.)

Adrienne said I needed to get a screen like she has to
separate her bed from her little brother's bed. She said
their apartment has two rooms besides the kitchen, but
her mom and dad had one whole room and she and her
brother shared the little room. Then her uncle made a
screen for her and that was much better. She took me
down to show her mother my bandage.

Her mother said she was so sad that my head was hurt.

She said my hair was very pretty and it would grow back nice where they had to cut it for the bandage. Then she said I shouldn't ride that scooter anymore and how my mother should know what a bad toy that scooter is for a young girl. She was really upset about that and went on talking about it to herself and shaking her head.

Adrienne showed me her own bed with the screen around it. It was almost better than a real door. It made it look private and secret and cozy. I decided I was going to have a screen like that around my bed, too.

We kneeled on Adrienne's bed and leaned on her windowsill. You can actually talk to people and see everything just like you're down in the street.

We could see our super, Benny Portelli, helping the man who drives the special big white truck. The truck only comes on Fridays to take away old furniture no one wants anymore.

And then my special thing happened to me. Suddenly I got lucky again! My mother says the fairies must have come when I was born, just like in the story, to bring me their special gifts. She says one of them must have brought me good luck, because over and over anyone can see that I am one really lucky kid.

And I am, too. At that very minute Mr. Portelli was handing a screen to the garbageman in the back of the truck. It looked a lot like Adrienne's screen, with wood all around like a picture frame and red cloth.

"Wait . . . Wait, Benny . . . Mr. Portelli! Wait!" I yelled.

"Excuse me!" I yelled to Mrs. Thieu. I had to really race through their kitchen.

"Your head!" Mrs. Thieu called after me. "Your head!"

I could feel my bandage sliding down over my eyes, but I ran right over to Benny.

"Mr. Portelli!" I remembered my mom said I should say "Mr. Portelli." "Don't throw away that screen. Please. Please, I need it."

"You want it?" He held it out to me. "It's yours. Just don't let me find it out here tomorrow."

Adrienne came down to help me take it up to my house. It was not an old thing at all. There was nothing broken or torn. It was very dusty, and the wooden frame was scrappy looking. Adrienne helped me clean it all up. I set it around my bed. Adrienne said I was an amazingly lucky person.

When my mother came in, she agreed it was the perfect thing. She kept hitting her head and saying she didn't know how come she never even thought of a screen for me.

I told her how I saved it from the garbage truck just in time.

17

"Because you're lucky," she said. She hugged me. She started to cry. She fussed getting my bandage straight. "You were lucky you didn't break your head," she said, "Elana Rose Rosen."

On Saturday, she took all the cloth off the screen, and I scrubbed it. Then we could see how pretty and bright it really was. She tacked it all back on the frame tight with special new brass upholstery tacks. She sent me to see if Mr. Portelli had a little upholsterer's hammer we could use, and I helped her hammer in the tacks. Then I made my sign.

EVERY DAY SHE RIDES HER SCOOTER

LOVES TO DANCE AND LOVES MUSIC

ADMITS SHE ACTS STUPID AND STUCK UP SOMETIMES

NOW SHE HAS FRIENDS AT MELON HILL HOUSES

AND NANETTE IS COMING

READING, WRITING, HISTORY, & GYM
ATE AS HER BEST SUBJECTS

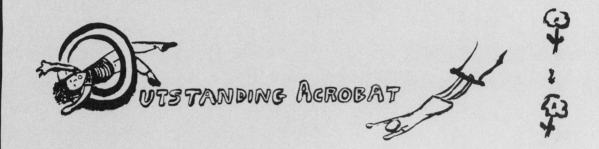

OUTSTANDING ACROBAT

SANDALS ARE HER FAVORITE KIND OF SHOES
KIRTS THAT SWIRL ARE HER FAVORITE KIND

EATING IS A FAVORITE THING [BUT NOT SOFTBOILED EGGS]

REALLY DREAMY TOO, SOME DAYS

OUTRAGED WHEN PEOPLE MAKE FUN OF GIRLS
R TREAT SOMEONE MEAN BECAUSE OF RACE
R ON ACCOUNT OF THEIR OPINIONS
R BECAUSE THEY ARE DIFFERENT

STILL WISHES HER DAD DIDN'T GO MOVE AWAY
O FAR WHEN SHE WAS JUST A LITTLE KID

EASY TO MAKE HER CRY REAL TEARS
SPECIALLY IF SOMEONE TURNS SARCASTIC BUT SHE IS

NEVER AFRAID TO SAY WHAT SHE THINKS
IN AN ARGUMENT

5

Petey is my shadow!
Everywhere I go he goes too.
Talks not at all!
Especially fun to play with.
You could love him lots!
You could get mad at him too!

A WEEK AFTER my accident, I met Petey for real.

When the elevator door opened to let me out on eight, he was standing there. He followed me to our door. His shoelaces were untied, and he had to stop and wiggle his shoe back on. I waited for him. I was sure he was the little kid who saved my scooter. I thought maybe he was five or four like my twin cousins. But they can tie shoes.

"Can't you tie your shoes?" I asked him. He wouldn't answer. "What's your name?" I asked him. He wouldn't tell me that, either, but he nodded when I said "Petey?" And he nodded again when I asked was he the Petey who saved my scooter. While I was bending over trying to unlock our door, I could feel him touching the bandage on

my head. It's just a small bandage now, and the doctor will take out the stitches tomorrow.

He followed me right in. On Tuesdays, my mom doesn't get home from her school and her job till just before supper. I was glad Petey was there. We went and looked at my bandage in the bathroom mirror. I took him in to see the scooter. The handlebars were high for him, but he stood on it just like he was riding it. I showed him the great features of this particular scooter. I held it up a little so he could spin the wheels and watch the silver and blue stripes blur. I let him help me polish them.

He never even said anything the whole time. I asked him if he could talk. He polished very hard but he didn't answer.

Petey came next door to Cecelia's with me. Cecelia is how come we found this apartment. She was a friend of my mom's a long time ago, even before my mom got married. (She even knew my father.) Cecelia works at the supermarket, but only part-time. When my mom gets home late, Cecelia is usually home. I go there, and she gives me a snack. We do puzzles and play Scrabble. She has fish and a big parrot that talks, and she has plants in cans all over the windowsill and hanging up. I am teaching the parrot new words. But Petey was scared of the parrot. Very scared. He stood in the corner and never

moved his eyes from that big bird. And he never said anything.

Cecelia told me in the kitchen that as far as she was informed he never did say a word. But she couldn't say for sure if he could or not. She gave us both glasses of cranberry juice and told me where to take Petey back to his baby-sitter, Mrs. Greiner, down at the other stairs on nine. That's how I first met Mrs. Greiner and got a job.

I help Mrs. Greiner take care of Petey. Because he runs and runs, and she complains she's much too slow and much too fat for that. She wears special furry slippers. They don't do much for her because feet such as hers are beyond help, she says. But she finds Petey real smart and quick. "Turn around and he's gone! Turn around again and he's back!" Mrs. Greiner just loves Petey. She's crazy about him. She'd be sad if she couldn't be Petey's baby-sitter. So I do the running after, and she does the looking after. I listen to her complaining. I do errands for her. Besides baby-sitting, she strings beads for people when their necklaces break. And I'm the delivery girl.

Don't think it is an easy thing to restring beads the way they were. It isn't. You have to make a knot between each bead, and each knot has to be in the exact right spot.

Mrs. Greiner tried to teach me, but my knots never came out in the right place. So then she told me she could see that I was meant to be a messenger, <u>not</u> a knitter or a knotter or any of those things.

But she can do all of those things very fast: knit and crochet and embroider and fix broken cups and earrings and carve teeny animals from wood.

And you can't always tell about Mrs. Greiner. When she's busy she won't stop for anything. But when she feels like it she tells long stories about when she was a child. And she has a lot to say about Melon Hill Houses, <u>and</u> the borough <u>and</u> the city <u>and</u> the whole world. . . . But she has a lot of things that hurt her besides her feet, I think. She says when it's hot out she can hardly move and when it's cold her bones can feel it bad. And wind gets to her. And rain. And when the news is bad it puts her off her food.

But she doesn't make good things to eat. Petey doesn't like to eat at Mrs. Greiner's, and neither do I. Petey likes to eat at my house. One time after she had been talking at me the whole morning about Melon Hill Houses not being kept up nice anymore and about things she read out of the newspaper about people who have nowhere to live and about how much fake pearls and those necklace clasps cost . . . I decided I better just go home. She has a special sad voice when she says all those things. It makes me feel <u>I</u>, Elana Rose Rosen, better do something right

away about the mayor and the price of beads . . . and housing . . . whatever . . . immediately!

The next time I walked up the stairs to her apartment, I made up a nickname to call her.

REALLY LOVES HER
ELANA RUSE ROSEN
NO WONDER THAT
IS AN UNUSUAL LADY
HAS NO T.V. IN HER HOUSE
WINS AT SCRABBLE MOST TIMES

EVERY SHAPE AND EVERY COLOR
HAS THOUSANDS OF BEADS
TELLS THE GREATEST STORIES

RUMBLES IN HER STOMACH AND WE LAUGH
EATS THINGS SHE SAYS AREN'T GOOD FOR HER
NEVER GIVES UP WHEN HER WOOL TANGLES
IS ALWAYS TALKING POLITICS TO EVERYBODY
ESPECIALLY ADORES PETEY
RAINY DAYS MAKE HER FEET HURT
GUESSES RIDDLES AND GUESSES WHAT'S BOTHERING YOU

SHE CAN JUST FORGET I'M A KID AND NOT A GROWN-UP
REALLY NICE TO ME BUT A LITTLE UNPREDICTABLE TOO
MAKES LUMPY SOUP, BURNED TOAST AND RUNNY EGGS

Once Petey made soup with me. I'll tell you about that weirdest soup we made. First I have to tell you how Petey's mother went in the ambulance to the hospital for an operation and about Petey's sky blue hat that he would never take off. And I have to tell you about Nanette coming to visit. It's hard to know what to tell first and what to tell after that. My mom says you should keep the best for last when you tell a story. I think the best should come first.

So first, before I tell about the ambulance and Petey's sky blue hat and the soup we made and Nanette's coming to visit, I'll tell about the sign that is now up in the lobby of 514. Adrienne says there's one in 515, 516, 517, and 518, too. Cecelia says there's one in the supermarket.

I was the first person who saw that sign, because I was standing right there when Benny, I mean Mr. Portelli, put it up. I held the tape for him. He is the super for all our buildings, and he takes care of <u>everything</u>.

The sign is just an announcement. It has no pictures. It says in big letters:

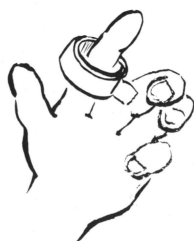

BOROUGH-WIDE FIELD DAY

Open to all children
between the ages of 5 and 12

MELON VALLEY PARK AND STADIUM

9:00 A.M.   LABOR DAY   SEPT. 2ND

* * * * *

GAMES * RACES * CONTESTS

RUNNING RELAYS * JUMPING * NOVELTY RACES

SKATES, SKATEBOARDS, SCOOTERS,

BIKES, TRIKES, PEDAL CARS AND CYCLES,

DOUBLE DUTCH AND ROPE SKIPPING

OTHER RACES TO BE ANNOUNCED

EVERYONE WELCOME

Join us for a day of picnicking,
band music, ball playing, frisbeeing,
and somersaulting

For more information and permission forms,
contact Parks Department

We are all going to get permission slips and sign up. I know Siobhan and Beryl and Adrienne and Vinh are going to. Eduard for sure! Jimmy Beck I guess. We may not want to be in a race with <u>him</u> because he talks so big, but it's a public park, Mrs. Greiner says. And he's a fast runner to have on a team.

Maybe Nanette can come and stay till then and be in it, too. It's real lucky it will be at the end of the summer, because Petey will just be five then, and it does say you must be over five. And we hope hope hope that Petey's mother will be all better then. She says she'll come, even if it's a sacrifice, for Petey's sake. But Petey's father says he's not so sure she'll be able to. They'll have an argument, no question about that! As you can often hear from way down the hall. Sometimes I wonder if my father and mother were like that, too. It's entirely possible. Maybe I could ask Cecelia. I can tell my mom doesn't like to discuss my father. . . . "<u>Mr.</u> Rosen, you mean," she always says in her most sarcastic voice.

WILL IT BE OVER

OVER

REALLY OVER.

R

IS

EVERYTHING GOING TO BE

DREADFUL FOREVER?

ALL OF US KIDS were playing in the courtyard. We heard the ambulance siren from far away, but we are real used to that because of Melon Park Hospital. Then we heard the siren so loud we put our hands over our ears, and a

Melon Park ambulance backed right up into the courtyard till it was practically on top of the benches. And before the siren even stopped, the ambulance people in their white suits jumped out the back. They said they were looking for 2H.

But 2H is where Petey lives! We all crowded around them. Mr. Portelli came rushing over to take them up in the freight elevator, and we followed them. But a police officer drove up in the police car right after the ambulance. She told us we had to stay back and make room and wait.

We waited and waited. Then we saw right from up close it was Petey's mother they were bringing out on their stretcher. She was covered with blankets, but we could see her face. She even smiled at us a little bit, that peculiar half way she smiles at Petey a lot of times. But her face <u>was</u> white. Right behind the stretcher came Petey's father. His face was real red. He was running and pulling and dragging Petey by the arm. Shoes and toys kept dropping out of his shopping bag. Petey tried to run back for his monkey doll that dropped, but his father was yelling at him that there was no time. Then Petey's father saw me, and he picked Petey up and stuck him in my arms so I almost fell over, and he dumped the shopping bag in Eduard's arms. "Please," he said to us. He was

30

panting from running. "Please take Petey up to Mrs. Greiner." He said it was all arranged and he'd phone her from the hospital as soon as he could with news.

The ambulance man reached down and helped Petey's dad up into the back of the ambulance to sit with Petey's mom. Then he shut the doors, and the siren started up so loud we all jumped back. We watched the ambulance and the police car racing down Melon Hill as far as we could. Past the supermarket, even. We could hear it for a long time after that. And then it was completely quiet in the courtyard. I was still holding on to Petey.

Petey was crying on my neck, and my T-shirt was wet. I took him up to Mrs. Greiner's like his father said to. Adrienne came up with me and brought the shopping bag of Petey's clothes and all his little stuff. I was hoping she could do something to make Petey laugh; usually she's good at jokes and funny faces. But she didn't do anything but look worried.

Mrs. Greiner knew about Petey's mom. She said she always knew she was a <u>sick</u> woman. But she said to tell her all the details. So we did, about the ambulance and how we could even see a little inside it and about the police car and about how Petey's father plopped Petey right in my arms so I almost fell over backward. Petey sat on Mrs. Greiner's lap. His head kept

31

slumping over onto his shoulder, and Mrs. Greiner kept sitting him up and hugging him. Then he fell asleep for real, and she put him in the corner of the sofa.

Mrs. Greiner's sofa is practically her whole house. She does all her beads and all her work right there on her sofa. Lots of times she has to lift out the sofa pillows to find her scissors or her little jeweler's pliers. But she keeps all her other stuff in the bedroom. She has cardboard boxes and boxes in there. She says you can't depend on anything and if she has to move she'd just as soon be packed up and ready to go, as people think old women like herself are an unnecessary burden. She came back out with a big pink bedspread with little tassels all over and tucked it around Petey. She wrapped him right up to his neck. She said that it was the least she could do for him to make him feel safe even though it is hot out.

Adrienne and me walked down the stairs real slow, all the way from the ninth floor. "Don't you think Mrs. Greiner the Whiner is a nice lady?" I said to Adrienne.

It was so suddenly bright out in the courtyard we could hardly see at first. Then we saw all the kids were in the monkey bars. They weren't even climbing, just sitting or kind of hanging. So we went over and sat, too.

It was bad. They were all talking about dying and who would die first and who would die next and after that and

after that. . . . It was really <u>sad</u>.

Eduard said wasn't it awful sad that maybe Petey's mother was going to die. Siobhan said well, you wouldn't really die from a tumor. Jimmy Beck said his grandmother died of that, and it was a sure thing that Petey's mother was going to die . . . that really she was probably dead already, or she wouldn't have looked so white. That was what it meant to look like that, he said. I told him he shouldn't even say such a thing and he didn't even know. He just loved to always say the worst thing he could make up and scare us all. He said what did I know, anyway, and that his uncle was a doctor. So he did <u>too</u> know! Adrienne said we shouldn't fight when Petey's mom was sick like that. Vinh said Petey's father was very mean to yell at Petey. Siobhan said she bet Petey's father was so worried about Petey's mom because you wouldn't want your wife to die. I said I would die if my mom died. Adrienne said she would, too. Siobhan said her daddy could take care of her if her mom died. Then Eduard and Adrienne asked the same question. "What if <u>both</u> your parents got killed in a plane crash? What could you ever do then?"

So then Jimmy Beck had to start in. He had to climb up so fast to the top of the bars he even stepped hard on my hand. Then he shouted down to watch out, he was a bombing plane, and he jumped down and ran around with

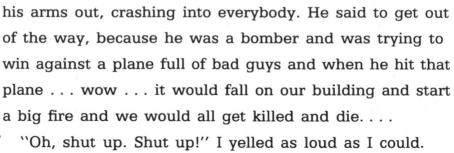

his arms out, crashing into everybody. He said to get out of the way, because he was a bomber and was trying to win against a plane full of bad guys and when he hit that plane . . . wow . . . it would fall on our building and start a big fire and we would all get killed and die. . . .

"Oh, shut up. Shut up!" I yelled as loud as I could. "Shut up. Shut up. Shut up, Jimmy Beck!"

"Bully!" Adrienne yelled at him. "Petey's mother is not going to die."

I went up to my own house and called my mother at her morning job. I told her about the ambulance and about everything. I started to cry. I told her Jimmy Beck said that Petey's mother was going to die. I asked her to tell me if Petey's mother could really die from her sickness.

My mom made me stop crying and listen to her. She explained to me about the operation. She said that the doctors and the family were almost positive Petey's mom would get well. She said she didn't want me moping around. She told me Jimmy Beck was bad news, just like she thought from the beginning, and the best thing would be to go up to Mrs. Greiner's and help her baby-sit Petey. She promised to call me later at Mrs. Greiner's and come home right away after her afternoon class. Then we could all come down to our house, and she'd bring home something nice for us.

34

"Cherries," I said.

"We'll see," she said.

"Watermelon," I said.

"I'll see," she said.

"Peaches," I said.

"Oh, you!" she said, and hung up.

7

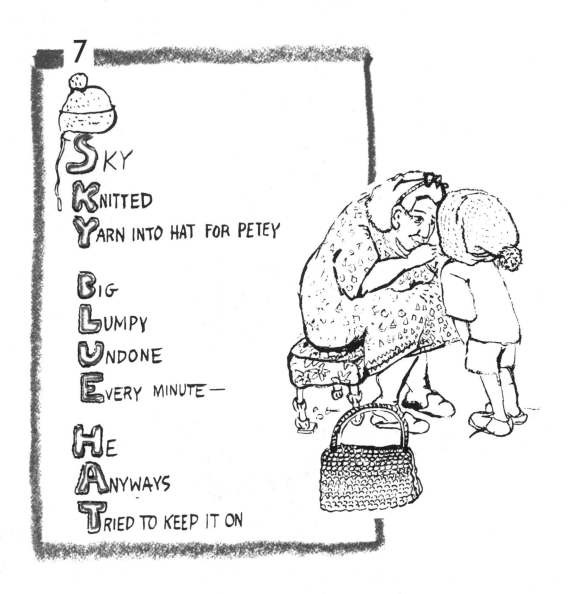

SKY
KNITTED
YARN INTO HAT FOR PETEY

BIG
LUMPY
UNDONE
EVERY MINUTE—
HE
ANYWAYS
TRIED TO KEEP IT ON

Mrs. greiner had on her outdoor shoes and her raincoat over her pink nightgown. She had a pocketbook made all of colored wooden beads. Petey sat in Mrs. Greiner's lap. And he was wearing his new hat. It did look like a winter hat, because it was woolly and had a pom-pom. I went with Petey and Mrs. Greiner to buy it.

36

Mrs. Greiner was telling my mother all about the operation Petey's mother was about to have on her stomach. I could tell Petey just couldn't stand for her to drag out all the details about the surgeon and the knife and the stitches and the anesthesia. He kept trying to put his hand over her mouth, and she kept pushing it away. She told all about her own gallbladder operation, too. And then she even told about her own mother's car accident! Petey kept shaking his head, which made the blue hat slide down over his eyes and nose to his chin.

"See, Mr. Petey . . . the storekeeper was right," Mrs. Greiner told him. "That hat is much too big. But of course we didn't have much choice because they don't really sell woolen hats in summer. Besides, that little store never has much in the way of choice," she explained to my mom. "We wanted to buy him a nice red summer baseball cap to cheer him up, but he wanted this blue woolly thing, and that's the only one the man had left." Petey started to cry.

"Well, there's no sense in crying, pumpkin eater," she told him, rolling his hat back up and tying it tight under his chin. "Just keep rolling it up and tying it. But don't you lose it. I spent my hard-earned bead money on it, and money is hard for an older person to come by these days."

37

Petey looked so very little in his big woolly hat. He looked so worried.

"Come down with me, and I'll take you on my scooter," I whispered through the hat into his ear. I could tell Mrs. Greiner the Whiner was getting Petey down.

"It's clouding up," my mom said. "It's going to pour."

"Just for a little," I begged my mother. "Just so Petey can get a good ride."

Mrs. Greiner walked over to lock the door behind us. She hugged herself around and shivered. "I hate these summer storms when it gets dark and cloudy like this so suddenly. It makes me feel blue," she said. "Blue . . . blue . . . like my time is over."

The courtyard was empty. All the kids had gone up. The wind was blowing papers around. Benny was bringing the garbage cans in so they couldn't roll over. "It's going to storm," he said. "Does your mama know you're out?"

"She said just for a little while," I told him, "so Petey can ride." Petey got on the scooter in front of me and I kicked off. We coasted around and around. No tricks. No jumps, nothing like that. Just around and around the courtyard.

The wind died down. It was quiet, too. No trucks. No sirens. No loud radios from upstairs. It was like

38

holding your breath. And suddenly Petey said something.

He said it very, very low with his head bent way down into his T-shirt.

"Say that again," I said. I put my face right down close by his face. "Tell it to Lanny again," I begged him.

We were halfway around the courtyard again when I heard him say, "This blue hat is a magic hat," and that was exactly what I thought I heard him say, and that was the first time I ever heard him say <u>anything</u>.

"Are you going to wear that hat every minute till your ma comes home from the hospital all better?" I asked him. He nodded.

"Are you even going to wear it in the bathtub?" I kidded him. He laughed.

"Even to sleep?"

He laughed more.

"I bet your daddy will make you take it off when he comes in to say good-night," I said. "He'll worry that you might suffocate in it."

Petey's father is a nervous person. And he's always losing his temper, too. Petey put both his hands on the sky blue hat and squashed it down tight on his head and held it there while I slowly rode him around and around the courtyard. The rain fell onto us and stuck in big drops on his hat. I wanted him to start to talk. I rode around

again and again, hoping he would say something. But he didn't.

I kept riding him around, though. Mrs. Greiner and my mom were probably sitting upstairs discussing problems of life and how life was hard, and I knew Petey didn't want to hear and neither did I.

8

PLEASE MAKE PETEY'S MOM GET BETTER FAST

LET HER COME HOME VERY SOON

ESPECIALLY DON'T LET PETEY GO AWAY

ALL OF US WANT PETEY TO STAY

SOMETIMES THE WORLD IS MEAN

EVEN IF THE REST OF THE WORLD IS MEAN
ELANA ROSE ROSEN WILL BE LOYAL AND GOOD TO PETEY

I promise
Elana Rose Rosen

PETEY'S MA WAS sick a long time. Even after she came home it took a long time till she was all better. A visiting nurse came in to help her every day.

One time while she was still away in the hospital,

Petey's father rang our bell looking for Petey. I was drawing at our table. My mom was studying. She told him Petey was up at Mrs. Greiner's getting his hair cut. Petey's father said good. He didn't think Petey needed his head covered with curls in addition to his other handicaps. It just shows how mixed up Petey's father is to say that.

Petey's dad stayed talking to my mom by the door. They saw I was listening, so they talked very low. I could hear them anyway. I heard Petey's dad sighing. He said he couldn't keep on much longer working and running all over trying to take care of Petey and maybe it would be better for Petey to be in a foster home till his ma got back and got all well.

My mom told Petey's dad that everyone in the building was glad to help out and that Mrs. Greiner was very good to Petey and taking the best care of him.

"But she's not a well person herself. She's got swollen feet and rheumatism, and she's not firm enough for a kid like Petey," I heard him say. "And I can't stay at home. I've got to go to work. And Petey is a handful. And if I go to pieces and get sick, too . . ." I saw him wipe his eyes with the back of his hand, but even so a tear ran down his chin.

I put my head right down onto my drawing paper.

After I colored it in, I sat looking at it. You always have to color a little more even after you're sure it's all done.

My mom came over and was standing behind me undoing my barrette and then fastening it up again. I tell her she's like that big old mother gorilla we used to watch in the zoo near Nanette's. I mean that way she starts to play with my hair whenever she gets near enough. Nanette's mother does it, too, and now even Nanette's biggest sister. I tell my mom the real reason she had me was so she could play with my hair! She said she knew I just loved it.

I do love it when we're alone like now.

"Do you like Petey's father?" I asked her. She'll never say yes or no to that type of question without thinking a lot. (That is a difference between grown-ups and children. I could . . . or Nanette . . . any of my friends could answer just like that.)

"Yeah, I do. I do like Mr. Timpkin," my mom finally said.

"What do you like about him?" I asked. I was coloring in the P very hard now, and I didn't look around. Me and my mom have lots of conversations that way. She says she knows what I'm thinking just from the back of my head, and now I can tell she's not so sure about Petey's father just from her fingertips stopping in my hair.

43

"What do I like about him?" she repeated. "Well, he does love Petey."

"But he doesn't look after him very well," I said.

"Uh-oh, a budding social worker . . ."

"You know what I mean. He doesn't stand up for Petey."

"It's his mother doesn't stand up for him! But you don't agree. I can tell," she said. See what I mean about this kind of conversation?

"But Mrs. Timpkin is sick. She's sick a lot," I told her. Actually I was thinking it was bad luck for my mom to be criticizing Petey's mom right while she was lying in a bed in the hospital. It might even make her not get better, and she had to get better for Petey.

My mom made one last big gathering of my hair and snapped it into the barrette as if she was saying, "Period. End of the conversation."

I agreed. The only thing to do now was color my message in bright enough so it would do its work, not leaving even the tiniest bit uncolored, not even the background. I fitted the completed message in the windowpane facing out . . . downhill and right at Petey's mom in Melon Park Hospital.

9

PETEY DOESN'T
*EVER
TALK
EVEN WHEN HE WANTS TO.
Y?

I TOLD MY MOTHER I knew Petey <u>could</u> talk if he wanted to.
My mother asked me how I knew. "I just know," I said.

"Well, how come he doesn't, then?" she asked me.

"Because . . . ," I said, "he kind of can't."

"But you just told me he could." She was upset. Then

Not exactly true anymore!!!

45

she was quiet. Then she asked me how I knew.

"A person can just tell," I said.

My mother came over and stood right in front of me. "Tell me the truth, Lanny. Did Petey ever, even once, say anything to you? And don't just say something and then say the opposite. This is a serious matter. It's not for your fa la la and fairy tales."

I went and stood up on my scooter. I looked into the sky. I <u>had</u> wanted to tell my mom what Petey whispered in my ear about his sky blue hat being a magic hat. I had wanted to tell my mother. Only I couldn't tell my mother because now I was inside Petey's secret. Besides, I just can't tell my mother <u>anything</u> when she sounds like that and gets like that. As though I didn't know it was serious whether Petey can talk or not talk. How could my own mother think I wouldn't know what was serious?

I could tell my cousin Nanette. I couldn't wait for Nanette to come . . . for them to decide if Nanette <u>could</u> come and for there to be <u>enough</u> money to get her a plane ticket. I had a million trillion quadrillion things saved up to tell Nanette, and one of the most important was to talk all about Petey.

When I was in bed that night, I heard my mother talking to Mrs. Greiner on the phone about Petey and whether he could talk or not. I heard her ask Mrs.

Greiner if she was sure the doctor had really said there was nothing wrong and to give her an honest short-form opinion . . . not tell her all about the problems of speech-lessness. My mom and Mrs. Greiner have become very good friends now. My mom says Rachel Greiner is both wise and true-blue. And they agree about politics and women's rights. Whereas Cecelia, who is a really old friend who my mom loves, doesn't care to talk about such things at all.

After she hung up, my mother came in and said Mrs. Greiner told her that Petey had been to a couple of doctors, and they all always said there was nothing wrong with Petey's ears or his voice box or his mind or anything like that. And she and Rachel Greiner didn't think there was anything wrong, either.

"See," I said to my mom. "I told you Petey could talk."

My mother convinced Petey's father to let her take Petey to a special doctor at the children's clinic who helps children who have trouble about speaking. I went, too, and waited with my mom in the waiting room. I leaned on her lap and read my book a little. I could see just under the curtains in the window, and I could see Petey and the doctor sitting on the floor together playing with a lot of different dolls. Petey looked like he was having a good time.

47

After, we went to the park. Petey ran ahead of us. He got to the big lawn called Gretel Green and started to somersault. He looked so cute, tumbling over his blue pom-pom. Petey is going to win the somersault race, and I'm going to win the scooter event. I told my mom so.

"How do you know that?" my mom said.

I ran over to Petey, and we both did somersaults till we were red in the face and my mom yelled at us to stop or we'd get sunstroke. Then I said to my mom, "I know because I believe in things. I believe we'll win, and I believe Petey can talk."

10

SAUCE MADE OF TOMATOES OR CANNED TOMATOES...
OUP CUBES...
ALT, PEPPER, BAY LEAF, PARSLEY ...

ONIONS, CARROTS, CELERY, POTATOES, MUSHROOMS,
THER VEGETABLES TOO....
NLY BE SURE TO CUT THEM IN SMALL PIECES
R CHOP THEM UP [WASH THEM FIRST].

USE 4 CUPS CUT-UP VEGGIES [FULL CUPS].
SE 6 CUPS WATER.
SE LEFT-OVER RICE, NOODLES CHILI, MEAT,
CHICKEN, SPAGHETTI......

PUT THE RAW STUFF IN YOUR POT OF WATER.
UT ON THE STOVE AND COOK TILL ALMOST SOFT.
UT IN THE LEFT-OVERS AND COOK TILL HOT.
UT IN MORE SEASONING IF YOU NEED TO.

Petey making soup is a joke.

And me and Petey making soup is a joke, too. I never
even made soup except just to help my mom. But I told

49

Petey I'd try to do it that day because he was so hungry and his mom still wasn't all well. She was home, but she had to rest. Besides, she seems to get tired of Petey a lot. Mrs. Greiner had a rush order to finish, restringing pearls for Adrienne's big sister's wedding, and she complained she couldn't stop to cook. She couldn't stop even to eat. We don't like how she cooks, anyway. And Petey absolutely won't, <u>won't</u> go to Cecelia's since Cecelia's parrot grabbed his hat.

Our own fridge and cupboard were very empty. By Friday most everything good to eat is gone. It's the day my mom gets her pay and takes me to do the shopping. Lots of times now she takes Petey along and does their shopping, too, to help out. I get us all cleaned up, and we wait downstairs for my mom. Then, every time, when we're on our way to the store, she says, "It's Friday night, kids, so how's about let's stop at the Blue Tile Diner and have ourselves a treat first?"

Petey always points to the french fryer for his order. It's the ketchup he likes. What he really likes is <u>squeezing out</u> that ketchup. Every time, we have to clean him up all over again before we can go shopping. And every time, Josephine at the cash register says, "Hey . . . whenever you bring that kid in here I know I'm gonna lose money. He costs me about a gallon of ketchup."

50

But on this Friday, my mom called from her job and said she'd be late and just to go next door so Cecelia could give us a snack. And to be sure to be ready on time and waiting downstairs. She was on a tight schedule.

Petey would still not go to Cecelia's though Cecelia makes good things to eat. Still he was very hungry, and I was hungry, too. We finished all the peanut butter and all the crackers. We scraped out the honey jar. Petey began to cry.

"Well, I can't make food out of nothing," I told him. I was so tired of him. I wanted to be outside on my scooter . . . moving fast! He went and stood right in front of my mother's big blue speckled pot she keeps on the stove. It's always on the stove because it's too tall and too fat to fit on any of the shelves. And because it's lived every single place we've lived.

Petey's blue pom-pom came close up by the pot, and he stood there just like he was listening to the pot . . . as if the pot was talking to him and he was listening. His blue pom-pom made him look like he belonged to the pot—a messenger for the pot. He went and got out two of our bowls and took two of our soupspoons out of the drawer. He gave me a bowl and spoon and stood with his bowl and spoon right in front of the pot, waiting.

"Oh, come on, Petey. You quit that," I scolded him.

"That pot's just a pot. It's just a plain ordinary empty pot! There's no soup or anything to eat in it, so there's no reason to stand there with your spoon and an empty bowl! Anyway, it would be much better if you would just say what you wanted!"

Petey did not listen to me. He was standing on a chair, pouring bowls of water into the pot. He was crying a little bit. He makes an awful noise. It scares me, because he sounds just like he's choking.

I wished my mom was there to make us soup, but I decided if Petey and me were really going to make soup we needed to do it right. I took his bowl and set it on the counter and rolled up his hat and tied it tight so it wouldn't be sliding down over his eyes all the time and the strings wouldn't get in the soup. I got him to wash his hands. I sponged up the water that was spilled on the floor. Then I emptied the pot and started us all over again.

"One bowl for you," I said. "One for me and one for my mom. Is that right?" I asked Petey. He pointed upstairs. "One for your mom and two extra for seconds?" I guessed.

Petey carried each of the six bowls of water to the pot and poured it in very carefully. And each time I saw him looking very specially at the big blue speckled pot. Then

he came over and whispered something up in the direction of my ear.

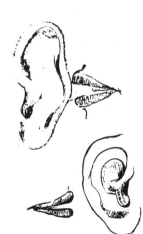

"What?" I asked. I picked him up so his mouth was right by my ear. "Tell Lanny," I said.

"It's a magic soup pot," he whispered. I could feel his warm breath tickle my ear.

"Tell Lanny more," I said. "Tell me what you mean."

But that's all he would tell me. After that he was getting things and getting me to get things to go in the pot. He brought the salt and then the pepper, too. He went to turn on the stove. I'm not allowed to turn on the stove, so I went next door and got Cecelia to do it.

Then Petey knocked loud on the fridge door. I opened it. To me it seemed very empty. But Petey pulled out three limp carrots and a half stick of limp celery. He found an end of cabbage and a little jar of leftover chili and one with rice and peas. He looked under our sink and found three potatoes in a bag and a big onion that was starting to grow. It had long sad-looking yellow-green leaves, but the onion part seemed okay.

Petey wanted to just dump everything in. But I knew we had to wash the vegetables and cut everything up. It was a lot of trouble, too, because my mom keeps her really sharp knife up high. I'm not supposed to use it. Petey liked emptying the bowl of little cut-up carrots and

celery into the pot. He kept running back and getting more from me as fast as I cut it. And I found a can of tomatoes I opened for him to put in, too. He plopped that in, and it splashed on his nose. That made him laugh. He got so excited. He wanted to put in more things.

He was looking in all my mom's little boxes of spices and seasonings. I knew it was good to put in those big dried leaves called bay leaves because my mom puts one in her soup. Petey floated one bay leaf in . . . then he let go another and another. I grabbed the box from him before he shook a hundred leaves in.

Petey kept bringing over more of the little spice boxes. He wanted to empty them all into the big blue pot. But I smelled them first and read out the names: cinnamon, nutmeg, allspice, ginger. . . . To me they smelled and sounded like pudding and cake and pie, not like soup.

Petey didn't care. He was running back and forth with anything he could find for the soup. He brought pickles.

"No, not pickles," I told him. He laughed and brought mayonnaise.

"No-o-o, not mayonnaise," I told him, and he laughed and brought mustard.

"Petey, not mustard!" I yelled. So he brought paprika, and I put in a few shakes. He brought soy sauce, and I put in a spoonful. But then he brought hot peppers.

"Not hot peppers!" I said. No way hot peppers in my soup. He brought baking soda, coffee, brown sugar, and tea.

"Petey-y-y!" I yelled. "That's enough!" But he ran and got soap powder, shampoo, machine oil. He forgot he was hungry. He was pulling things out of everywhere and bringing them to his magic pot. He was laughing and laughing. I was laughing and laughing. "How about socks? De-licious sock soup . . ." "Crayons and marbles . . ." "Shells and pebbles . . ."

11

Makes Me

Answer Too Quick—

Dumb and Smart in One Body

"What's going on in here? You know you're not supposed to turn on the stove when I'm not home!"

There stood my mom. I could tell by how she was looking around at the jars, boxes, and cans Petey and I had spread out everywhere that she had come home without much sense of humor.

"I can't believe this mess," she groaned. But then she got mad. "This is the single worst mess I ever saw!

I come home tired from school and work. . . . I expected you to be downstairs ready to go like every Friday. . . .''

"Petey was hungry," I explained.

"Petey was hungry." She was mimicking me, and I can't stand when she does that.

"Is that a reason for such a mess, Elana? You're supposed to be the older one . . . the responsible one."

"I was responsible," I insisted. "I did get Cecelia to turn on the stove, and Petey was hungry and he wouldn't eat at Cecelia's, and Mrs. Greiner was busy, so I made soup."

Petey climbed up on the chair by "his" pot. He lifted the lid for my mother and held out the ladle to her. I saw her make a face. (I didn't think that was so responsible . . . to hurt Petey's feelings.)

"We didn't really put in all those things," I told her.

"No shampoo?"

"No shampoo, no machine oil, no socks, no hot peppers, no chocolate or coffee or tea. Really," I said. "Not even ginger or cinnamon or brown sugar."

I started to carry some boxes back to their shelves.

My mom stirred up the soup and stared way down into it. She took a little taste. Then another. She asked me to say exactly what we did put in, and I told her.

"It'll be okay, I guess," she said. "But it isn't hardly

cooked enough. Didn't you know soup takes long? You
kids, you put all this stuff away . . . every bit of it, fast,
so we can go do the shopping.'' She was in her hurry,
hurry, hurry state. I got the feeling maybe we wouldn't
have such a good time that night.

She grabbed a handful of macaroni, some dried parsley,
and kept stirring so fast the soup splashed up.

"Well, I'll tell you one thing, Elana Rose Rosen, if this
turns into really good soup, this has got to be a magic
pot,'' my mom said.

Petey climbed up on the chair again. He put his mouth
almost right into my mother's ear.

"It's a very magic pot,'' I heard him whisper.

My mom picked Petey right off the chair. She gave him
a big hug. She swung him around. "Did you hear that,
Lanny? He can talk,'' she said. "Can't you, sweetie?''
Suddenly she seemed less grim, and Petey was smiling
at her.

"Didn't I tell you he could talk?'' I said. But my mom
didn't seem to be hearing me. She didn't even listen to
me. She just kept looking at Petey and being amazed.

I tried again. "But I told you Petey could talk.''

She turned quickly to me. "Oh, don't always be so
concerned with what you said. It's Petey's own
accomplishment. Run get washed. This Friday we'll really

have something to celebrate at the Blue Tile. And get that new green shirt I bought you . . . for Petey to wear. His has got food all down the front."

I ran my eyes up and down and around Petey, measuring him. And for the first time, he looked very small and not too cute. "My shirt is not going to fit him," I said.

"Don't be petty. We'll roll up the sleeves," my mom answered. "You, you're always putting your clothes on Petey anyway!"

Well, if I wanted to put my clothes on Petey, that was one thing. He was my friend. He wasn't a doll for everyone to just try things on and praise one minute and ignore the next. . . . I stood looking in the bathroom mirror, brushing my hair. My mom called to me to hurry, that Petey was hungry.

And suddenly there it was. Mad. I couldn't hardly bear how mad I felt . . . so mad and mad so fast. Usually I have a little voice inside me warning, "Uh-oh, Lanny, something is going to go blooey."

Wasn't I the one who knew in my special inside kind of way, from the first day I met Petey, that he could speak? Wasn't I Petey's absolutely best friend? Didn't I just go and make that whole soup (when I really wanted to be outside scootering around) because he acted so hungry?

And now my mom was telling <u>me</u> Petey is hungry and giving him my shirt I was intending to show off at the Blue Tile tonight. How could my mother possibly be a friend to Petey like I am? Even Mrs. Greiner isn't. Even Petey's own mom isn't. So how could my mom imagine she knew all about Petey from his saying just one teeny sentence? And I didn't like her voice today. Somehow she came home tonight not with her usual voice but with that other voice she had.

"What are you doing in there, Elana? Did you fall in?" she yelled through the bathroom door, shaking the doorknob.

"I'm not going," I said.

"Open that door," she said. "I can't discuss anything with you through a locked door, and I have no patience for tantrums tonight."

I pushed the door open with both hands. "I <u>am not going</u>," I said. "Go with Petey!"

Petey started to cry. I made up my mind to not hear Petey cry, to not see his sad face.

My mom lifted Petey up. He hid his face on her neck like he had made up his mind he better stick with her if I was going to dump him.

"You're making your little friend feel just awful," she said to me.

Now did I need her to tell me that? I could feel from right behind his eyes to right behind mine how bad he felt at what I was doing and how he <u>wanted</u> to be on my side but couldn't because I wouldn't let him be. And Petey would not like for my mom to call him "my little friend."

I smacked the hairbrush hard into my hair at the side of my part and pulled it slow as I could to the very tip of my hair while I watched him. But I used a look I have, a little bit sideways look, to wipe him right out of my life even while he was right there in front of me.

My mother had an expression on her face that made her face be not even her own face, like her voice was not her own <u>real</u> voice. She stood there and shook her head.

"You're like your father," she announced. Amazed and disgusted is how she sounded. "Just like your father. <u>Stubborn</u> and <u>sulky</u> and <u>uncaring</u>!"

Petey had slid down from my mother's arms and came close to me, almost standing on my shoe. He didn't care if I was like my father. He wanted me to be <u>his</u> Lanny again and to come to the Blue Tile Diner just like every Friday. I longed to come. I loved how we all walk into the diner together holding hands.

My mother was cruel to be acting like this, making it so I just <u>couldn't</u> go to the diner with her and Petey and

61

celebrate when I <u>wanted</u> to do exactly that, go with Petey and her and sit at the counter and order stuff.

"I bet my father went away from you because you were so rotten and unfair and mean to him, too, even though he really wanted to stay with me," I screamed at my mother.

Words rushed out of my mouth and there was no way to turn them around and swallow them back in. I didn't even want to.

"Elana!" my mother roared, and at the same minute her hand shot out and hit my cheek hard.

I turned right back into the bathroom and kicked the door shut behind me. Then I heard the slam of our front door.

I listened to them walk down the hallway—they didn't come back. I waited for them to get down to the lobby and call me up . . . but the phone didn't ring.

The room got very, very quiet.

12

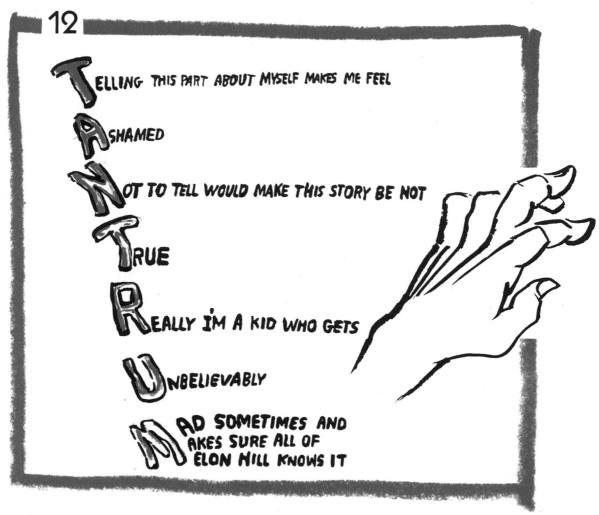

TELLING THIS PART ABOUT MYSELF MAKES ME FEEL

ASHAMED

NOT TO TELL WOULD MAKE THIS STORY BE NOT

TRUE

REALLY I'M A KID WHO GETS

UNBELIEVABLY

MAD SOMETIMES AND
MAKES SURE ALL OF
ELON HILL KNOWS IT

I WHACKED THE DOOR. . . . I tore it open, I screamed out into the empty hall, "I don't care if you never come back." I slammed the door. I pulled it open and sent another "Never!" after the first one down the hall. And another. And slammed the door.

In between, I had to stop to catch my breath and to

63

hear if maybe Cecelia or <u>someone</u> would come . . . come and stop me from having this tantrum. I only heard the awful parrot flying from wall to wall.

I haven't had a tantrum (only almost) since we moved here. I thought I had left them behind at Grandpa and Grandma's now that I am older. I tried going and standing on my scooter and looking out the window. There was one of those magic pink-cloud sunsets. But once my mouth opens and tantrum words start pushing out, there are a hundred thousand million more words crowding out my face . . . out my arms . . . my legs.

I shoved the window up. "Stupid sunset!" I screamed to it. Down on Melon Hill Avenue, I saw Petey and my mom mixed in with all the people going to do their Friday night shopping.

"I DON'T CARE!" I yelled at their backs. And they stupid heard me! How could they <u>not</u> hear me when I was just about breaking the sound barrier? But they didn't even stupid turn around.

"I HATE YOU-U-U!" I let go into the atmosphere, and slammed the window down. But I pushed it up again. "And that goes for all the rest of you, too!" I ran into the bathroom.

"And I hate you, too," I hissed at my face in the mirror over the sink. I pulled my hair all this way and out that

way. "You're ugly!" I screamed at my face. "Ugly . . .
ugly . . . ugly . . . ugly. And your father is ugly,
too, just like you!"

Tears started up at how ugly me and my father are and
how he never can even come . . . probably because of my
mom! Yes! Because of my mom!

I went right over to my mother's bed and her dresser,
and I pulled open every drawer in the dresser and then
every drawer in her bed—those are the big drawers—and
even though I was crying, I pushed and pulled my hands
through everything: her underwear and her blouses and
the winter covers and the sheets and towels and her
beads and scarves and I never stopped a minute till I
found the big tin box of family photographs.

I knew my mom had put it somewhere in there when
we moved in.

I kneeled by my mom's bed and I spilled out all the
pictures on the bed.

There was my father . . . my father and Megog (from
"My dog" when I was too little to say it right. Grandma
and Grandpa have Megog now). There was the house
where we used to live, with vines growing over a porch.
There was my baby carriage. There was my mother with
her hair all long before she cut it, holding me looking
over her shoulder.

65

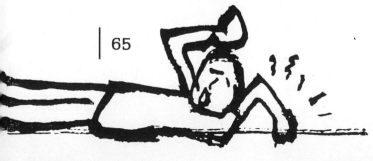

I set out all the pictures of my father in their own row.

I reached down my mother's hand mirror from her dresser.

My father and I have the same nose. I have a lot of hair. He doesn't have much. I'm tannish skin and little freckles. He's tan with big freckles. He has a mustache. I crossed some of my hair over my mouth to make myself a mustache.

The pictures don't tell me anything like why did my parents get separated and why doesn't my father write. How come he only saw me twice again after we moved away and how come he doesn't send us any money except on my birthday and once in a while some other times. That makes my mom so upset . . . so upset she won't really explain things.

And I can't get real details out of my grandma. The first time I ever saw most of these pictures I was sitting on my grandma's lap. I asked her about the beautiful house with the vines and if we could go and live there again after we lived with her and Grandpa.

Grandma got so serious then she scared me half dead. She pushed the pictures all away and put her arms tight around me. Though I tried to get down off her lap, she wouldn't let me. She said I must listen to her and always, always remember what she was telling me—that I would

66

never live in that house again, but I would live in lots of places and make lots of friends and no one in the whole wide world could ever tell all the wonderful places I would go and all the wonderful things I would do. She made me say it right along with her: ". . . all the wonderful places I will go and all the wonderful things I will do . . ."

Later when I stayed with Nanette, I recited that to her all serious and solemn like Grandma said it to me. Nanette said it gave her little shivers but she loved to say it like a secret password on the streetcar when we were going to a place we never went before.

I started to cry so hard and so loud for Nanette.

How I wished Nanette could live in 8F, right next door. How I wished my mother would get home. I put my head right down in my mom's pillow that smells of my mom's perfume and cried and sobbed till the pillow was wet and my mouth was full of fluff from the pillow cover.

And right then the phone rang. That's either because our phone is a phone that can understand, or because I'm still a lucky girl (even in the middle of not being so lucky).

"Come home soon!" I begged my mother, trying to catch my breath and not cry more.

She said she'd done the shopping, and she just had to

walk back up the hill and take Petey to his apartment, but if I wanted she'd take a cab and be there in five minutes.

"It's too expensive," I told her. Funny how sometimes my mother just _forgets_ about money. Over the phone I heard her doing something noisy. It turned out she was blowing her nose and dropping packages, and then she lifted Petey up because he wanted to make a kiss for me into the phone.

I guess I fell asleep, because later my mother was just there. I didn't hear her come in. She was sitting by me on her bed, wiping my eyelids with a cotton ball dipped in something cool. She undid my shoes, and I shook them off and wriggled out of my jeans.

She tidied the bed and pillows and collected up the photos. When I asked her could she leave those pictures out to look at, she set them in a row on the bookshelf. She switched off the lamp and put on the little night-light. And I watched her putting the groceries away in the half dark.

I asked if Petey had ordered his usual french fries and ketchup tonight. She said of course, but he only ate a few, and he got Josephine to wrap up the rest for me.

So half-asleep I ate half-warm fries while my mom got ready for bed.

"Shove over, you great huge girl," she said to me when

she had her nightgown on and her hair brushed out.
"You're taking up the whole bed!" So I squinched over by
the wall and made a big place for her to get in the bed.

"Not that far, silly goose," she whispered, and pulled
me over close.

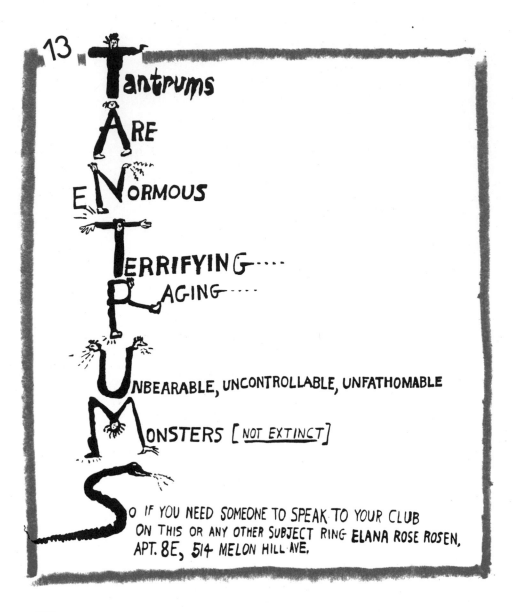

13 Tantrums

Are

e**N**ormous

Terrifying·····

Raging·····

Unbearable, uncontrollable, unfathomable

Monsters [NOT EXTINCT]

So if you need someone to speak to your club on this or any other subject ring ELANA ROSE ROSEN, APT. 8E, 514 MELON HILL AVE.

THE NEXT DAY while my mother was at work I made this acrostic for her. Unfortunately I got peanut butter and jam on it because I love to draw and eat at the same time. But she liked it a lot anyway. She put it up by her bed.

14

Oh Look how Dirty...

How All worn out This old blue hat!

PETEY'S SKY BLUE HAT got so dirty it got sky gray. But I never saw him without his hat till his mother was completely better and out of bed. Neither did my mom. Neither did Adrienne or Siobhan or Vinh or Jimmy Beck, though Petey held on to it tight whenever Jimmy Beck

71

was around. Benny never saw him without it, either, and he kept good track of everything in every corner of Melon Hill Houses. And Mrs. Greiner and Cecelia all said they never did. Really I did, and Cecelia and Cecelia's parrot did for a little while.

The parrot yanked it right off Petey's head one day and sailed and swooped from the wall to the window with it. Petey is afraid of that parrot, but he fought and screamed and jumped up and down and hopped around till the parrot dropped his hat. He was crying like anything, but he put his hat right back on. I rolled it up and tied it for him.

By the time Petey's mother was all better and out of bed, almost everyone in Melon Hill Houses had a chance to tie Petey's sky blue hat on for him and roll it up.

Right after Petey's mom got better, she put the hat in the wash with Petey's dirty clothes. She said it had food and clay and mud and she didn't know what on it. When she took it out of the dryer it was stiff and tiny from the heat. It had shrunk. I took Petey up to show Mrs. Greiner how little the hat was, sitting up on top of Petey's head.

She said people didn't know anything to wash a genuine woolen hat that cost good money in scalding hot water and then put it in the dryer that is the ruin of woolen things. But then she laughed.

"Well, you're lucky, anyway, Mr. Peter," she laughed. "Any way you look at it, you're lucky. Number one is, your ma got all better. Number two is, it's August now, and if you didn't need a hat in July you certainly don't need one for the dog days of August. Number three is, Adrienne's ma, Mrs. Thieu, is going to have a baby and you can give it to Adrienne for the new baby."

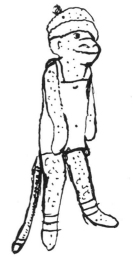

I knew Petey would never give the sky blue hat away. One day I watched him try it on his monkey doll made from a sock. It didn't fit right. He pulled and yanked at it to get it down on the monkey's head. Then he started to pull at an end of the blue wool that was sticking out. He pulled it out into a longer and longer string of wool. He pulled faster and faster, and I turned the monkey round and round for him as he did it. The strand of blue wool got longer and longer and the hat got littler and littler till only the pom-pom was left.

Petey kept the pom-pom in a jar. He took it out sometimes and played with it. Then it rolled away somewhere. Mrs. Greiner showed us how to make a new pom-pom.

HOW TO MAKE A GOOD FAT POM-POM *by Rachel Greiner*

BEFORE YOU START, FIND YOUR SCISSORS, SOME THIN CARDBOARD [BUT STIFF], A BALL OF YARN, A YARN NEEDLE, A PENCIL ...

① **CUT TWO SAME-SIZED CIRCLES OUT OF CARDBOARD.**

  you can draw around the top of a glass (or the bottom) for your circles, or use a compass.

② **NOW YOU HAVE TO CUT HOLES OUT OF THE MIDDLES OF THE CIRCLES LIKE A DONUT.** Draw around a nickel for a good round hole.

③ **THREAD A YARN NEEDLE WITH YARN & PULL IT DOUBLE.**

  I always start with about a yard (3 ft.) of the yarn.

④ **NOW HOLD YOUR CARDBOARD DONUTS TOGETHER LIKE A SANDWICH.**

  You'll need to wind yarn all around the rim of the donut like this:

  Start your needle up through the hole. Hold down the yarn ends against the cardboard for a few turns till it holds.

⑤ **GO ROUND & ROUND UNTIL THE HOLE IS SO FULL OF YARN YOU CAN HARDLY PUSH YOUR NEEDLE THROUGH.** Take new lengths of yarn as you need them. *DON'T BE LAZY!* Wind close together!

⑥ **CUT THROUGH THE YARN ALL AROUND THE CIRCUMFERENCE OF "DONUT." SLIP A LONGISH PIECE OF YARN BETWEEN THE TWO CARDBOARDS.**

  Wind it a few times and tie it tightly. Leave the ends long. Tear away all cardboard.

⑦ **NOW FLUFF OUT YOUR POM-POM.** Trim it evenly all around and sew it to your hat by the long ends of yarn. You should have a good fat pom-pom like the one Petey lost.

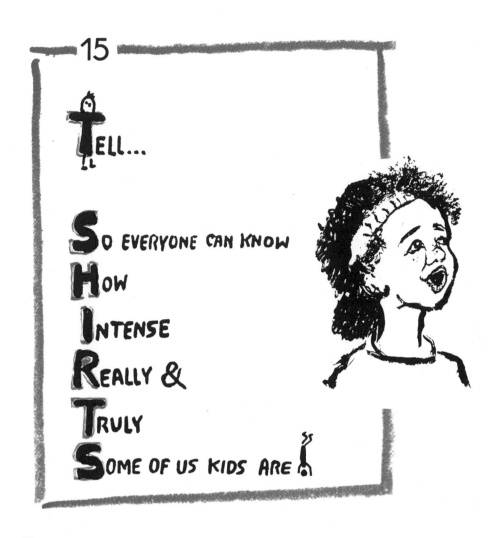

15

Tell...

So everyone can know
How
Intense
Really &
Truly
Some of us kids are!

Jimmy beck and petey and Siobhan and Adrienne and
Vinh and Eduard and me, too, colored on the pavement of
the courtyard. Jimmy had this great idea to write it so big
you could read it from the eighth floor. But it turned out
you couldn't really because we didn't have enough chalk
to color it in strong enough, it was so huge.

Benny promised he wouldn't wash it away for two whole days. That's when Nanette is coming.

And now there's going to be a meeting in the community room of the Melon Hill Houses. This meeting is for everyone. It says so on the bulletin board. It was my mom and Mrs. Greiner who made up the notices. I went with my mom to her college, and we got copies made for the other buildings, too.

The plan is, my mom says, to get everybody together to put in money so all the kids from all the Melon Hill Houses can have matching T-shirts for the Field Day. Then we'll be like a team.

On the bulletin board are our names and pictures. I helped Mrs. Greiner make a page for each of us on cardboard (she liked my printing so much). That way, she said, everyone could see it was their own neighbor kids who were going to be in the Field Day, so they'd want to help get the T-shirts and then they'd want to come watch.

Adrienne's mother knows a company that makes T-shirts for bands and clubs and all. They sell them wholesale. She's going to find out how much it will cost, and maybe they won't cost so much as they usually do because she can buy them for the wholesale price.

I told Mrs. Greiner we would have to get a special small T-shirt for Petey, otherwise it would come down

over his knees and he'd get all tangled up doing somersaults. Mrs. Greiner said I was a worrier like herself and
that was why we got on so good, but that she would fix it
for him if it didn't fit. She said if I wanted something to
worry about, I should concern myself with the possibility
that Petey's stomach would turn permanently upside
down and the blood would never return to his feet
because he was practicing somersaults so much. But
when I asked my mother about this, she said Mrs.
Greiner was a tease. Sometimes I don't like that Mrs.
Greiner so much. Mrs. Greiner the Whiner, the Tease.

I wish we could have real rose red T-shirts, and the
writing should be black or maybe pink. Pink would look
beautiful on the rose red. But so would the black. Every
color looks beautiful with rose red. If you try it out you'll
see I'm right.

My mom says we won't be able to choose colors,
though. Because that would make each T-shirt cost way
too much. "Anyway, you kids could never agree about the
colors. Right?" she said. She was laughing because I had
a great big argument with Adrienne about which red was
really rose red. I believe there is only one perfect rose red.

♠ Eeek, watch out for his skate board!
Don't get in his way!
Unbelievably fast!!
Amazingly tricky!!
Reckless friend!
♠ Daring, danger-loving Eduard! ♠

♣ Best team captain!
Expects us all to win!
Relay races are her favorites!
You have to see her in action!
♣ Loves an audience too!

♣ Very high jumper

In the playground or street

No one jumps higher

"Hey come watch me," says Vinh

Just one fast runner-
Is on our team-
Makes big steps-
Moves legs fast-
"**Y**ou be there to watch me," Jimmy says.

Extraordinaria
Lista
Animada
Noble
Atlética

Quería usar mi español.

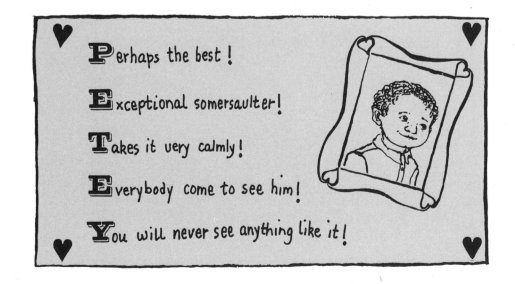

Perhaps the best!

Exceptional somersaulter!

Takes it very calmly!

Everybody come to see him!

You will never see anything like it!

Says she can't jump far.

Is too modest, we all say.

Our building is all for her.

Broad jumping is her sport.

Has long legs

And strong too.

Never a quitter.

No one here knows Lanny's cousin yet.

All of you will like her.

No doubt about it.

Especially fast runner.

Taking a plane to arrive soon.

Then she'll be on 514's team.

Everyone come to see my cousin Nanette run.

♣   ♣   ♣   ♣   ♣   ♣

Alright!

Double Dutch fiend!

Runs fast too!

Is never without a jump rope -

Every day she practices -

"Next time a hundred,

Next time five hundred", she says.

Elegant!!

16

BECAUSE,
EACH
SOMERSAULT,
TEACHES PETEY TO DO THE NEXT.

M**RS. GREINER MAY** be right that we should watch out for Petey fainting from dizziness. He has turned into the wildest somersaulter. We've lost track of the number. I wish he hadn't taken apart his sky blue hat, because that could protect his head. (Mrs. Greiner says I should talk when I'm the one who had an accident to the head.)

Petey's father was laid off his job at the airport for a week, and he took Petey down to Melon Valley Park a lot. I went with them on Wednesday. Petey's father made him somersault a way where he crosses his feet as he lands so he is doing his next somersault immediately. He got Petey to do it over and over perfectly. We kept track on the sidewalk up to thirty-five, and then we lost count.

We lost count because the big geese that live in the pond by Gretel Green came up onto the grass and were walking right at us to check if we had bread. Petey's father lectured us that geese were not harmful animals. But a person knows for themselves when to be afraid or not afraid, and once where I used to live a goose bit on my little finger so hard it turned black.

So we really don't even know how many somersaults Petey actually did do.

17

SONG OF OH HOW LONG? NANETTE

I AM AN ESPECIALLY LUCKY human being. One time I walked in my sleep, and I went right out our door. But then I rang Cecelia's bell and went in her door . . . all in my sleep. My mom says it was just another example of that luck of mine that I didn't go walking out a window. When I had my scooter accident, my mom said I was lucky to get a taxi driver who got me to the hospital fast as an ambulance, almost. I'm really lucky I have my grandparents. My grandma is always sending me funny postcards, and it was Grandma and Grandpa who gave me my scooter and are taking care of Megog for me. Jimmy Beck says I'm lucky I like to read, because he doesn't like it at all. Adrienne says I'm lucky I like to do cursive. She hates writing things down. Cecelia is always telling about how lucky Petey and I were that we didn't get stomach poisoning the way we made that soup. ''Experiment soup,'' she calls it. And she says I must be lucky with parrots, because the parrot likes me so much and that parrot doesn't like a lot of people. I was lucky to find my screen just the minute before Benny threw it out. Mrs. Greiner says as a messenger I have amazing luck because whenever I deliver the beads people always seem to be at home. My mom says she is the luckiest mom in the world to have me. I'm lucky to have my mother.

And now, I'm so lucky because Nanette is coming for sure. She is coming today! My aunt Anna just called to tell us when to meet her and the flight number. She called up very early because it costs much less to call long-distance that way.

After she called, I went down with my scooter. I wanted to see how far over I could tip, going in a smaller and smaller circle, without falling. It was still before

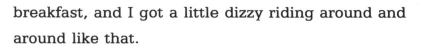

breakfast, and I got a little dizzy riding around and around like that.

So I went and sat on the bench and watched everyone coming out of our building on their way to work. It was nice out there. Benny was sprinkling trees with the hose. It was still cool and cloudy. I told him Nanette was coming and we were going to go to the airport to meet her. "You're a lucky kid," he told me.

"Do you think I'm what you would call unbelievably lucky?" I asked my mom when I was washing up the breakfast dishes. She didn't hear me on account of the water. She was listening to the weather on the radio and trying to decide if she needed an umbrella.

"Don't worry, it's not going to rain today," I said.

"Are you the new weatherwoman?" she asked.

"No," I said, "but Nanette is coming today. And I am an unbelievably lucky person."

"A what?" she asked.

"An unbelievably lucky person."

"You are <u>an unbelievable talker</u>," she said, and pushed me away. Then she gave me a big kiss. My mom went to work. And then I had the whole day to wait till we had to go to the airport at supper time.

I went next door to Cecelia and tried to teach the parrot to say "unbelievable." But it takes a long time to teach a parrot a new word. And you can't do too much at once, Cecelia says. She says that's the clue to success with parrots.

So I went and got my markers to work on a new sign. I wanted to make it look as if it was made of colored lights like the ones I saw downtown. Cecelia had an old pad of graph paper she let me use. It took a long time to make that sign, and still it was only lunchtime. Cecelia made

sandwiches, and I tried to see how long I could make my sandwich last. I cut it all into pieces. Finally, the last half of the last half of the last half of my bread was so tiny I licked my fingertip to pick it up. And the hands on Cecelia's wall clock hardly moved at all.

"I think your clock is broken," I told Cecelia.

"I think you better take your scooter and go down and play with the other kids," Cecelia told me.

It was too hot . . . much too hot to go out in the courtyard, I thought. So Cecelia said well, why didn't we surprise my mom by moving Cecelia's big chair that opens up into a real bed to our apartment next door and put it right next to the couch I sleep on and get it ready with sheets for Nanette.

So then it was all ready for Nanette. And I taped my sign on the door all ready for Nanette, too.

And still the clock had hardly moved.

So I went up to Mrs. Greiner's to see how her clock was doing and if Petey was there. Petey had gone somewhere with his mom, and Mrs. Greiner's clock must have stopped, too. Maybe something was wrong with the electricity in our whole building! Mrs. Greiner said nothing was wrong with her clock, but I think maybe her eyes aren't so good anymore from stringing beads.

18

SAY A STORY...

TIME JUST FLOATS AWAY

OR DOESN'T MATTER

REALLY ONLY THAT STORY MATTERS

IN THE MIDST OF A STORY

EVERYTHING ELSE

SEEMS SO FAR AWAY

Mrs. greiner was in a good mood. She had just washed her hair, and it stuck out all over like a whitish gray bush. She's much older than my mom, but when I ask her exactly how old she is, she always says, "Oh, that! Who cares about that?"

She kidded me because I was looking at the clock so

much. She gave me a glass of her fruit punch that is the only good thing she makes. It has jam and tea and pieces of orange and pieces of peaches in it. And I got her to tell me how to make it. I wrote it down so I could make it for Nanette. Still the clock wasn't working. Mrs. Greiner started to sing and hum. She taught me a song about a grandfather clock that stopped short never to go again.

She said if I'd sit by her and help her sort beads (that's usually Petey's job), she'd tell me a story.

I asked her what it was going to be about, and she said it was actually from the wonderful world of real life, her own childhood, to be exact. "And don't ask me this time if it has a moral," she told me, "because you should know by now Mrs. Greiner wouldn't waste her breath if it didn't."

When I was a little kid nothing I had matched: not my stockings (when I had stockings), not the buttons on my coat (when I had a coat), not even my shoes. My mother got the left shoe from one cousin, the right from another. I thanked my stars there __was__ a left and a right and not just two lefts or two rights to make me walk sideways, like a crab.

And believe me, my feet were better off than my hands. One hand had a mitten. The other had nothing. But it really wasn't so bad. I could put my hand that was red from the cold in my coat pocket. My coat pocket did have a big hole in it, but I found my way through the lining to an inside pocket that was in my skirt. That pocket was good and warm, and there I kept my hand while I was standing on the stoop of my building.

And let me tell you I stood on that stoop <u>a lot</u>, because we lived in a very crowded apartment. It was my mama and papa and seven sisters and brothers and my grandma all together. I remember that itty-bitty place. When my grandma first moved in with us, she said, "But this place isn't even big enough for a closet for a rich person to hang up all her fancy clothes—so how will there be room for me?"

But people old or young, rich or poor, and whatever they look like have to have a place to sleep . . . and a place to eat . . . and a place to pee, even if that was just a toilet in the common hall. So there my grandma and all of us had to live, and all I can say is thank goodness the roof didn't leak.

You've heard of wall-to-wall carpet? Well, in our place the beds went wall to wall, and still there was no way we could all fit in to sleep at night. But necessity worked out a way. My big brothers and my father worked at night, and my mother and my sisters worked all day—when they were lucky enough to find work at all, that is. As soon as one got out of bed in the morning to go to work, another coming home from work climbed right in, so the beds always remained warm.

In the daytime, we younger ones were shooed out onto the stoop. If we complained, my mother would say, "If you want to eat, then your big brothers and sisters have to get their sleep so they can work and earn money to pay the grocer and the landlord. At least if we pay rent we <u>have</u> the stoop." So . . . cold days, windy days, drizzly days . . . it was "Out of the house!" for us.

Of course the other young ones went to school. I wasn't old enough to go, so that left me with no one as well as nothing to play with. I was a real skinny little thing, too. I remember how Mama used to pinch my behind and look so sad and say there wasn't hardly enough there for me to even sit on. My grandma was always trying to sweet-talk the grocer into a little extra milk in our pail for me. Milk still came down from farms in milk pails then, and the grocer dipped it out into your own pail with a ladle. But as the grocer said, the whole neighborhood could use free milk, and then how would he and his make a living?

But sad facts like I'm telling you can add up differently than you think sometimes. And so it came about that I was noticed by a kind person on our block.

He was also a person that counted for something around there. He was the tailor, and he had had the shop across the street from way before I was even born. Any time I could, I watched him cutting out cloth, pinning up hems, sewing up seams. Then I would go whir, whir with a block of wood, playing that I, too, had a sewing machine and was doing important work like little kids do if you give them the chance.

One day the tailor came by, and he asked me what I was sewing so busy there. Another time he came across and right up on our stoop to bring me a remarkable cookie that had red jam in the middle. I've remembered that cookie for sixty years now, jam was such a treat to me then, if you can imagine.

Then one fine morning (there were fine mornings then, too, despite everything), he called to me when he came to open his

store. He said that he had something special for me and to watch out for the traffic and run across. Traffic then was still horses and carts, as well as cars and trucks. On our block alone we had the Pots and Pans Man, the Fish Man once a week, and sometimes the High-Cash Clothes Man. Horses don't go fast like cars, but they have big heavy feet, and you had to watch out. I saw several nasty accidents from my spot on that stoop.

But I went across, and what the tailor had for me was a long wooden box with carving on the front. He said he came upon it looking for something in his cellar. It was left over from one of his old treadle machines he gave up when he put the good modern one with the electric motor in his shop. Of course I mean modern for that time. What was up-to-the-minute then is old-fashioned now.

Of course I was standing there wondering (you're probably wondering, too) what use an empty drawer could be to a kid like me. But then the tailor started to pull things out of it to show me.

It was crammed full with spools of colored thread, wool yarn and embroidery silk, velvet and satin ribbon, beads, buttons, hooks, and you name it. There were even some little lace-covered buttons that I fell in love with right away. And among the packets of needles was one that had those big needles with the fat holes. I knew immediately I wouldn't have much trouble threading those. By the way, I never told you that even as a little girl I couldn't see too well. But people like us had no money for glasses. I got those much later when they opened up a free eye clinic in our neighborhood.

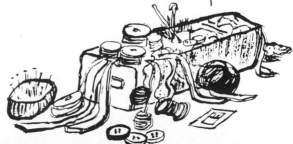

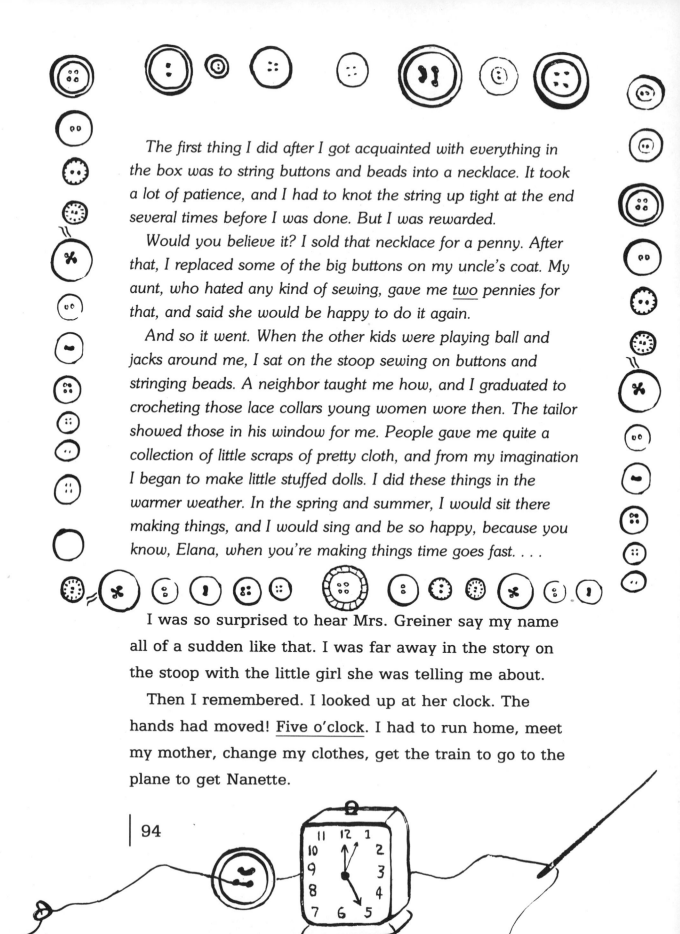

The first thing I did after I got acquainted with everything in the box was to string buttons and beads into a necklace. It took a lot of patience, and I had to knot the string up tight at the end several times before I was done. But I was rewarded.

Would you believe it? I sold that necklace for a penny. After that, I replaced some of the big buttons on my uncle's coat. My aunt, who hated any kind of sewing, gave me two pennies for that, and said she would be happy to do it again.

And so it went. When the other kids were playing ball and jacks around me, I sat on the stoop sewing on buttons and stringing beads. A neighbor taught me how, and I graduated to crocheting those lace collars young women wore then. The tailor showed those in his window for me. People gave me quite a collection of little scraps of pretty cloth, and from my imagination I began to make little stuffed dolls. I did these things in the warmer weather. In the spring and summer, I would sit there making things, and I would sing and be so happy, because you know, Elana, when you're making things time goes fast. . . .

I was so surprised to hear Mrs. Greiner say my name all of a sudden like that. I was far away in the story on the stoop with the little girl she was telling me about.

Then I remembered. I looked up at her clock. The hands had moved! Five o'clock. I had to run home, meet my mother, change my clothes, get the train to go to the plane to get Nanette.

94

19

NEVER NEEDS ME TO EXPLAIN

ALWAYS UNDERSTANDS

NEVER SAYS "WELL, I GUESS... <u>MAYBE</u>"

ESPECIALLY ENTHUSIASTIC

TRULY A FRIEND

TELLS ME HER OWN MADE-UP STORIES

EATS THE ICE CREAM, I LIKE CONES
EATS THE MEAT, I LIKE BONES

N**ANETTE LOVED** the silver and blue wheels on my scooter the minute she saw them. The morning after she came, we stood up on my scooter and looked out my window. It

wasn't really hot yet. A little breeze was blowing on us, and we were still in our underpants. It made her shiver, even though it was the middle of the summer.

It makes you shiver to be up so high and see so much sky and to see all those pigeons flying. You think the pigeons are high at the top of the sky, but then you see way higher even than the pigeons, airplanes are flying. And the airplanes look silver. And there are thousands and thousands of buildings all the way to the river. And the river is silver. And when the sun comes up, the windows of all the buildings on one side are gold like they're on fire.

Tomorrow we're going to get up early enough to see those windows be like they're on fire.

I showed Nanette all the bridges across the river and then way away farther, the bay. And I showed her how there were little tugboats on the bay and more bridges.

She asked me what were those wooden things pointed like farm silos that stuck up above the buildings. You could see them whatever direction you looked.

Water towers, I told her. That's where they keep the water for the tall buildings. Nanette said that's where she'd live. In a water tower. Only first she'd let out all the water.

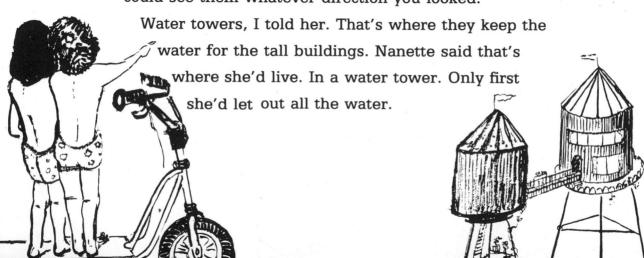

I knew Nanette would want to live in one of those
water towers the first day I ever looked out this window.
I had one picked out for us. I showed it to her, and she
agreed we should have a round bed in it, too, and a porch
and our own walkway to the other water towers, and we
said who could live in the other towers.

I showed Nanette everything in the Melon Hill Houses,
and we walked to Thieu's Variety Store (we had sodas)
and the library, too. That's the farthest I'm allowed to go
alone. And we played ball and tag in the courtyard with
Adrienne and Eduard and Siobhan. And then Mom took
Nanette and Petey and me to the Blue Tile Diner for
supper. And we sat at a table. And we had anything we
wanted that didn't cost too much. Only we didn't have
dessert, because we wanted cones and they only have ice
cream in dishes. We got our cones at Thieu's and made
them last exactly all the way to our front door.

Sunday morning we did get up early enough to see the
windows with the sun on them like they were on fire.

My mother said she guessed we could just kiss sleep
good-bye while Nanette was here, since we had stayed up
half the night telling stories and laughing and now we
were up at sunrise. She made us toast before she went
back to bed, and we each put our toast in our pocket and
took my scooter down.

97

The courtyard was absolutely empty. Sunday a lot of people in our building sleep late. I ate my toast while Nanette tried the scooter. Nanette ate her toast while I showed her some of my specials.

Then we rode around together.

At first we were real quiet, just gliding around.

But Nanette doesn't ever stay quiet for long, and I don't either. She asked me did I remember the big rubber factory near her house where her brother and our other cousin worked. I did remember it very especially, because it was an amazing big building that took up a whole block and it was made of maybe a billion bricks at least with a wall all around it, and it seemed like a million people went in through a gate in the morning and then came out the other gate at night. I would even have paid (but not too much) to go inside and see how they made all the things they made . . . all sizes of real high-bouncing rubber balls, combs, too. And gloves for doctors, all kinds of stuff, my other cousin told us. But I wanted to see the balls being made, because I could never even imagine how you could really make a rubber ball.

"Did you get to go inside?" I asked Nanette.

She said you couldn't because they didn't allow children in. But that she had a story to tell about it anyhow, because . . .

98

One time they forgot to turn off the machines and faucets of the great big tank where they cook up the rubber that comes from rubber trees in the jungle. So when the rubber was all melted it just kept running into the tank, then the tank got so full it ran out on the floor. Then it filled up the room and ran out the windows. Then it filled the streets up deep . . . up past the first-story windows and past the second-story windows and past the third-story windows.

"What about the people who worked in the rubber factory?" I asked her.

When those people who work there wanted to go home, they found that the doors and the windows were all blocked up with rubber. So they went up to the fifth floor, where the rubber didn't reach, and they jumped from the windows. It wasn't a big jump. Just like scaling that wall there.

That rubber was so bouncy that when they landed on it they bounced . . . and when they landed again they bounced even higher, and they bounced and bounced and couldn't stop bouncing.

We were turning the sharp curve then on the scooter at the up end of the courtyard . . . while she was saying, "Bounced and bounced and couldn't stop bouncing." Then I said as I pushed us around, "Bounced and bounced and couldn't stop bouncing," in time to my foot pushing. "And they could never ever stop bouncing," she said.

"Are they still bouncing?" I asked her.

"Still bouncing to this day."

"Is that true?" I asked her.

"Yes," she said. "And we have to bring food every day, and we have to hand it to my brother and to my other cousin the minute . . ."

I started to laugh and she started to laugh and we were laughing and laughing and laughing, and the scooter fell over so we were laughing even harder and louder.

Only then suddenly Petey's mother leaned out the window.

"Hey, you kids. What the heck's the matter with your brains? It's Sunday morning!" she yelled. "You stop that racket immediately or I'll call the police."

"Don't yell so loud!" we heard Petey's father yell to her from the other window, and she slammed the window down so loud Mrs. Thieu opened her window and looked out, too.

We had to laugh without making a sound. We laughed till we just about choked. I wish Nanette never had to go home.

20

LIKE TO MAKE

INTERMINABLE LISTS...

SURE IT'S SILLY SOMETIMES B<u>UT</u>

TOTALLY NECESSARY WHEN ARGUING WITH

SOME CERTAIN PERSONS ABOUT YOUR RIGHTS
O YOU WILL BE ABSOLUTELY
URE TO
AY EVERY
INGLE FACT YOU
AVED UP YOUR WHOLE LIFE TO
AY TO THEM !

W<small>E WERE STILL LAUGHING</small> when we were waiting for the elevator. It finally came, and there was Jimmy Beck. He made a face at us and pushed the D<small>OOR CLOSE</small> button

101

before we could run on. (We didn't even <u>want</u> to get on with him in the elevator.)

The elevator took forever to come back down, and we heard Jimmy laughing over by the fire-stairs door that he thinks is his private exit. So we figured he had taken the elevator to the top floor and pushed all the buttons, so the elevator would stop at every floor and we could just wait. He knows we aren't going to walk up eight flights. (Of course, he ran down the stairs.) I said we should go get him now so he'd know he couldn't push us around. Nanette said who cared, anyway.

I said I cared.

She said, well, don't care.

I said you couldn't just not care if you did care and that I always knew I'd have a fight with Jimmy Beck. She said what she meant is, we didn't have to do it <u>right</u> then, because we already had a million things we needed to do, starting immediately! When we got upstairs, we made a list on my grandpa's old typewriter that he gave me.

        ★ ★ ★ ★ ★
        ★   ★
        ★ 1. ★ Make pancakes for my mom to eat in bed
        ★ ★ ★ ★ ★ because it's Sunday. Nanette knows how with
                   blueberries.

        2.   Go to Thieu's Variety and buy a box of pink,
    ($ $ $)   blue, yellow, peach, and sea green chalks
                  Nanette really needs.

        3.   Go downtown with Mom and go shopping
                  for new school shoes for Nanette (her big
                  sister sent along $$ for her) and also for me
                  (as soon as $$ comes from Grandpa and
                  Grandma). Then show Nanette the Crystals
                  Room in the Museum of Natural History.

    @ @ @ @ @
    @   @
    @ 4. @ Get 6 new books from the library to read with
    @ @ @ @ @ Nanette (at least 6 because 2 of us together
                  read more than 2x as much as 1 of us alone).

        5.   Go with Adrienne and Vinh to show
                  Nanette the school where I'm going to go,
                  so they can show me the secret passage
                  that goes there.

    & & & & & &
    &   &
    & 6. & Go to the beach (<u>important</u>):
    & & & & & & A.   Go in the biggest waves with Nanette.
                        I. Take Petey, too.
                        II. To be decided when we get there.
                  B.   Go on the roller coaster!!
                        (Take Petey on the Ferris wheel.)
                  C.   Build the biggest drip castle yet with
                        Nanette.
                        (Petey, too)

7. Try making Mrs. Greiner-the-Whiner's fruit punch.*
   A. Also make pom-poms for Nanette to take home for my other cousins.
   B. Ask Mrs. Greiner to tell Nanette one of her great stories.

8. Take Nanette to speak French to Cecelia's parrot and see if he understands. Cecelia thinks so.

9. Baby-sit Petey for Mrs. Greiner, so Nanette can earn money for a present to bring her mom and dad.

10. Write a "BILL OF PARTICULARS" note to put under Jimmy Beck's door.

*Somewhere there's a recipe she gave me ...

My mom read this list and said we really could do almost all those things but we were just on a tear with this Jimmy Beck thing, though as she said from the beginning Jimmy B. is not a great specimen of humanity. Still, she said, we should consider what we ourselves are doing to be getting in these fights.

Nanette and I disagree totally and completely. We have evidence for everything on that list.

It is truly a Bill of Particulars. Someday Nanette and I will be a lawyer and a judge, and this can all be proved in court.

BILL OF PARTICULARS
* AGAINST JIMMY BECK *

1. JUST HAS TO MAKE SOMEONE
   FEEL BAD EVERY MINUTE!

2. IS ALWAYS TEASING SOMEONE!

3. MESSES UP MY SCOOTER!

4. MAKES FUN OF PETEY!!

5. YELLS AT EVERYONE!

6. BLOCKS EDUARD ON HIS SKATEBOARD WHENEVER
   HE CAN TAKE HIM BY SURPRISE!

7. EATS CUPCAKES IN FRONT OF US AND
   DOESN'T SHARE!

8. CAN'T EVER JUST PLAY AROUND EASY
   LIKE THE OTHER KIDS!

9. KNOW-IT-ALL!

10. THERE WILL BE ANOTHER PARTICULAR
    FOR SURE!

Rachel Greiner's
Summer Fruit Punch

We used to have this for a treat instead of canned juice or sodas which we couldn't afford. Besides my mother was suspicious of foods in jars or bottles from the store. She made her own raspberry jam for this drink and tea for the base.

I do it this way.

1) Rinse off and dry two (2) lemons and two (2) big juicy oranges. Have an extra lemon in case you need it.

2) Grate about ½ teaspoonful of peel (just the yellow, not the white part under the yellow) from one of the lemons and save on a saucer.

3) Squeeze both lemons and both oranges. Be sure you get out all the juice but do not strain it. Pick out all the seeds (don't be lazy) before you pour the juice into a pretty jar or pitcher.

4) Add the grated lemon peel.

5) Add three (3) cups of good cold water (or tea.)

6) Now add some pieces of the squeezed out oranges and a sliced up peach if you have one.

7) Add three to six (3-6) teaspoons (full) of raspberry jam according to how sweet you like it. (Strawberry or cherry jam is o.k. too but raspberry is best.)

8) Mix it thoroughly! Taste it and make it to your own taste. More jam will make it sweeter. Lemon juice or water will make it less sweet. (Water is good for you!)

9) P.S. I say put in ICE CUBES but Mrs. Greiner believes ice is bad for a person's stomach.

Elana

21

SWELL
WOW
OOOO
OOOPS
PLEASE
ENTERTAIN YOURSELF FOR A WHILE
DEAR SHADOW

NANETTE AND I bought a big box of colored chalk. Petey came with us to the store. We did not exactly plan to take him. We planned to <u>not</u> take him, because since Nanette came he has just about glued himself to me with magi-glue. But he came along anyway. Mrs. Greiner asked if we could just take him with us while she coped with some jewelry repair that required "one hundred and ten percent attention." She gave us money to buy something for him and to get oranges for her to make more fruit punch and some number five shoelaces for Petey's shoes. He had taken out the laces to tie them together to do string tricks and now no one could find them. It was slow walking down Melon Hill to Thieu's because we had to keep stopping for Petey to put his foot back in his shoe.

We wanted to go try our chalks without him. And Nanette said she had a new story to tell. We did the shopping, and Petey had enough money to get a little car (candy apple blue, his favorite color). It was even slower going back up the hill because of Petey stopping to try the car every smooth place we went by. We had to swoop him up the last part of the way, and we swooped him into the elevator. We swooped him to Mrs. Greiner, and we swooped him right onto her sofa. Then we tickled him so we could run out while he was laughing.

Mrs. Greiner says Petey is jealous since Nanette came, but she says he doesn't need to be because Nanette will go away again soon whereas Petey will continue to be here. When I reminded her Nanette was in fact my best cousin <u>and</u> my best friend, too, she said that was okay, that was good, but Petey was my shadow and no one in the world can escape from their own shadow. Then she said one of the poems she knows hundreds of: "I have a little shadow that goes in and out with me and what can be the use of him is more than I can see. . . ."

But I don't want to get away from Petey. It's only <u>today</u> that I prefer to do something alone with Nanette.

108

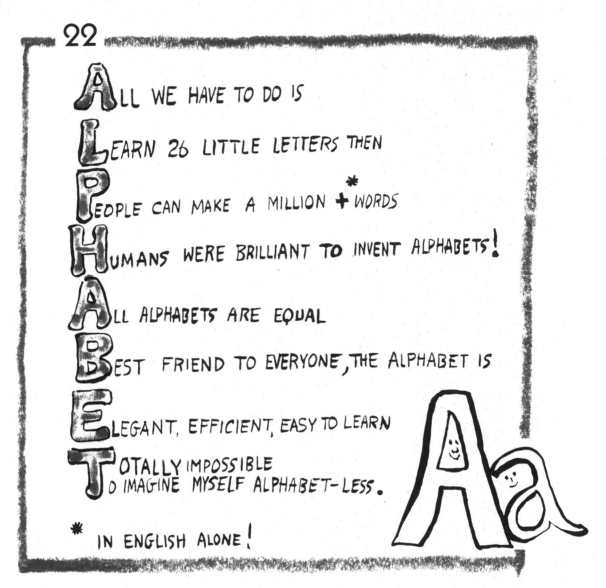

22

ALL WE HAVE TO DO IS

LEARN 26 LITTLE LETTERS THEN

PEOPLE CAN MAKE A MILLION + WORDS *

HUMANS WERE BRILLIANT TO INVENT ALPHABETS!

ALL ALPHABETS ARE EQUAL

BEST FRIEND TO EVERYONE, THE ALPHABET IS

ELEGANT, EFFICIENT, EASY TO LEARN

TOTALLY IMPOSSIBLE TO IMAGINE MYSELF ALPHABET-LESS.

* IN ENGLISH ALONE!

Don't you love it in the summer when it's so hot you can hardly move and you lie in the shade outside and you watch the clouds move and someone tells a slow story?

Nanette and I went downstairs with our chalk and

hairbrushes to dry our hair and brush it out and get it to go right, because yesterday we were at the beach and our hair got going all wrong. We got our favorite bench under one of the locust trees. Nanette said she'd brush my hair first so she could tell me a new story, because . . .

> *Once a boy was eating vegetable soup with alphabet noodles in it, only when no one was looking he took his bowl outside and dug a hole in the yard and poured his soup in. . . .*

"Why did he do that?" I asked.

"Because he wanted to see what would happen if you plant alphabet noodles," Nanette said.

"So what did happen?" I asked.

"You can't keep asking me or I can't tell the story right. And I forget to brush your hair. . . . I have to talk <u>and</u> brush at the same time for it to come out smooth," Nanette said.

"The story or my hair?" I asked.

"Lanny . . . don't be like that," Nanette begged.

"Okay," I said. And Nanette started over.

> *Once there was a boy who was a very curious type of kid. He wanted to be a scientist when he grew up. So he decided to do an experiment. And the next time he had alphabet soup for lunch, he got his chance. He sneaked out into the garden and poured the soup into a hole at the end of the row of broccoli*

plants. He had to sneak out because lots of times it's important to do experiments in secret until you are sure they are going to go right and not turn into some kind of awful goop or fizzle out.

He waited a whole week. He checked the spot every day, but he did not see even a little bit of a green stem or a single leaf or anything. He thought maybe it took alphabet noodles a long time to grow. But he decided while he was waiting it would be good to try the experiment another way. He thought that maybe cooking had made the noodles so they wouldn't grow. So he bought a box of uncooked alphabet noodles and planted those. This time he watered them. And he was careful to plant them on the night of the full moon. And he tried the end of the lettuce row in case the broccoli had had a bad effect on the first set of

(Nanette stopped brushing my hair at this part. I guess because this was such an important part of the story.)

This experiment was so stunningly successful it could not be a secret. Not only was there a huge tree where he had planted the alphabet noodles (he planted one of every letter in the alphabet and an extra set just in case some of the noodles were not good seed). But it was there the very next morning. His mother and father were standing there. They were just amazed at this tree. Because as you can imagine no one ever saw anything like it before since the world began. A whole tree to grow in one night! But that was nothing. What the boy's parents didn't notice at

111

first was that this tree had letters hanging from every branch . . .
every branch. They couldn't believe their own son had planted it.

"But where were the letters?" I asked Nanette.

"On the tree like I said."

"But exactly where? Were they like cherries or like
pinecones or did the twigs twist up funny?" I asked.
"And were they like printing or writing, and were they
like our alphabet or a different alphabet like Hebrew or
Russian or Greek or Chinese? You didn't tell about that."

"Well, what do you think? They were like the alphabet
we learn in the U.S. in school because that's what the
scientist planted. Later, after it became a famous
experiment, they tried other alphabet noodles from some
other languages in other boxes. And it turned out to be
just as stunningly successful, but that's not in <u>this</u> story.
Every single thing can't be in one story. . . . Did you bring
the box of chalk?" Nanette asked me.

I had it in the pocket of my shorts, so we went over to
that really smooth dark piece of pavement between 514
and 515. It's the best place to draw and it's shady there,
too. I drew the tree and Nanette showed me how the
letters looked on the tree . . . only she wasn't sure at all.

Written capital <u>S</u> is best, I said . . . and also the <u>L</u> and
the <u>R</u> and the <u>V</u> are beautiful if you write them fancy, but

not the E and not the A. Printed ones are more beautiful, I said. And I started to draw them right out of the ends of the twigs.

"But they have to be just like the noodles that he planted," Nanette complained.

"Well, cherries don't look like the seeds you plant," I had to tell her.

"But the cherry pits do," she reminded me.

I said I was the illustrator and the best thing was to make the letters that I thought were the most beautiful. She said they had to be true according to the story. I said no one had ever seen such a tree before, so how could she be so sure?

"Well, you're right about that," she said. "But I'm going on with my story."

And what happened is that the boy grew up and became a scientist, and he had to spend years and years figuring out how these kind of noodle seeds worked. And even though he lived to be very, very old, and they gave him the Nobel prize, he didn't ever get it all figured out.

"That's not such a great ending for a story," I said.

"It's not the end," Nanette told me. "This is the end."

This tree got to be a famous, famous tree. People came from far away to lie under the tree and look up. Thousands of poems

and stories were written looking up into that tree. And thousands
of songs, too. And if children had trouble learning to read they
could come there and learn easily. . . .

"Learn easily . . ." We heard a voice from behind
the bushes imitating us. "Learn easily . . ." It was Jimmy
Beck. He was laughing. He jumped out of the bushes at
us. Branches and leaves tore and scattered. He grabbed
Nanette's new double-size box of chalks and ran.

We chased him till we got so hot we were in danger of
heat prostration. Nanette and I agreed it wasn't worth it
to have our brains melt, even for a double box of chalks.
So we went up and got our suits and called for Petey and
came down to get cool in the playground sprinkler.

In bed that night I asked Nanette if she thought Jimmy
Beck was hiding in the bushes the whole time to listen to
the story.

"Do you think so?" she said.

"Do you?" I said.

"Well, do you?" she said.

"Well, do you?" I said.

"You two are driving me up a tree," my mom said.

"A tree?" Nanette said.

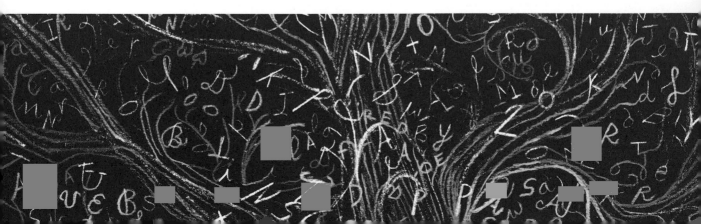

23

HOW CAN WE WAIT

OUT THIS NIGHT

TILL TOMORROW?

THE NEXT NIGHT was the hottest night.

My mom brought our supper down to the courtyard.
We ate corn and pickles and tomatoes at the checkers
tables.

All the kids were out. Everyone.

We were all running around and playing like it was the

middle of the day. Well, it was light . . . light almost as day. But not in that same way. It was a special light, and everyone knew it was special. It was a kind of light purple-blue light with a half moon floating up in it.

All the kids started to draw on the sidewalk. Jimmy, too. But we moved away from him. Then he brought out that same box of chalks he stole from us and laid it down right next to me and Nanette.

"Let's make an even bigger sign than last time, you guys," he said. "We've got enough chalk to do it this time. We've got Lanny and Nanette's box, and I've got a new box, too." He put the new box down with the other right next to us. Suddenly it seemed like everyone had brought chalk in their shorts and shirt pockets . . . all colors, too . . . real red and genuine blue and true, pure magenta pink . . . brilliant magenta pink!

"We're going to make a sign you can see from the moon," Jimmy shouted (so the moon could hear).

"From Mars," Siobhan shouted (so Mars could hear).

"They'll take pictures of it from a satellite," Vinh said.

Late at night Nanette and my mother and I crowded at our window in our nightgowns. We could read our sign eight floors below, and it was beautiful.

24

R EALLY ?

E XACTLY ?

A CTUALLY ?

D IRECTLY ?

Y ES..NO, YES..NO?

OUR NEW T-SHIRTS were spread on the chair. They were the color I wanted them to be, the color of a certain kind of rose—rose red.

We got all washed up and put on some of my mom's after-bath powder that I love to smell. Nanette likes it, too. With powder on us our new shirts slipped right on.

We went to call for Siobhan and Beryl. They had on

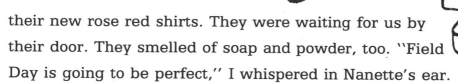

their new rose red shirts. They were waiting for us by their door. They smelled of soap and powder, too. "Field Day is going to be perfect," I whispered in Nanette's ear.

But when we rang Petey's bell and Petey's mother answered, she said they weren't ready yet. When we tried to remind her how everybody had agreed for <u>all</u> the 514 kids to go down to the stadium <u>together</u> but <u>early</u> and the grown-ups to come after, she said we were just making her ill again. Petey's father called from the back that they would get down there when they were able and ready to go. The door slammed shut right in our faces. Beryl made a horrible face at them through their door. I wished it could turn them to stone, except when it came to getting anywhere or doing anything they were enough like stone already. So we had to go to the stadium without Petey. That got us down, and we didn't race down the hill like we would have.

Even so, the 514 Melon Hill House kids were the first ones in the stadium. The park attendants were still fixing the big iron gates to stay open when we walked through. (Only I scooted through and Eduard skateboarded.) The grass smelled like it was just mowed. The big concrete stadium steps were washed and empty. On the bottom step, a band was unpacking its drum and saxophone and trumpet and other instruments and tuning up. I staked

out the best seats for my mom and Cecelia and the others, right in the middle of the third bleacher step. We put our lunches there and my scooter. The second the volunteers had the tables with the sign-up sheets ready, we all ran over to sign up for our races.

I signed up for both scooter events and the sack race. Nanette and Jimmy Beck signed up for two running races, the thirty-yard dash and the sixty-yard dash. All the 514 kids signed up as one team for the running relay. Adrienne signed up with Siobhan and Eduard as partners for the double Dutch, Eduard for two skateboard events. Vinh for the high jump, Siobhan for the broad jump. Nanette and me together for the three-legged race. Petey for the hopping . . .

But when we went to sign up Petey for the somersault race (we were worried that he wouldn't get down there in time to enter his name), we couldn't find any sign-up sheet for a somersault race. We went from one table to another, looking. All the volunteers who were helping with the sign-up said they had never been informed that there was going to be a somersault race or event of any kind.

Kids were just coming into the stadium now from all over the borough in all different colors of special shirts. The other kids from 515, 516, 517, and 518 Melon Hill

Houses had come down. We could pick them out everywhere by their rose red shirts, same as ours. And everyone in back of us was complaining at me and Nanette for holding things up, asking and asking about the somersault race.

25

SCARED....

EVEN TOO SCARED

TO TELL HER I'M SCARED

As soon as I saw my mom come in with Siobhan and Beryl's mom and Cecelia, I went and got her.

We went to find the director of the whole Field Day program. She had a walkie-talkie and a clipboard with an up-to-the-minute list of all the events. She told us it was complete. But there was no somersault race or event on her list, either. My mom and I took her over to the fence to show her where it said about the somersault race <u>right on the poster</u>.

And then we saw! We saw how <u>we</u> had really made the mistake! I felt so stupid. The poster didn't really and exactly and precisely say somersault race the way it said the other races. Here is what it did say, and you can judge for yourself if it doesn't kind of give you the idea that there's a somersault race. But I felt so stupid!

BOROUGH-WIDE FIELD DAY

Open to all children
between the ages of 5 and 12

MELON VALLEY PARK AND STADIUM

9:00 A.M.   LABOR DAY   SEPT. 2ND

✷ ✷ ✷ ✷ ✷

GAMES * RACES * CONTESTS

RUNNING RELAYS * JUMPING * NOVELTY RACES

SKATES, SKATEBOARDS, SCOOTERS,

BIKES, TRIKES, PEDAL CARS AND CYCLES,

DOUBLE DUTCH AND ROPE SKIPPING

OTHER RACES TO BE ANNOUNCED

EVERYONE WELCOME

Join us for a day of picnicking,
band music, ball playing, frisbeeing,
and somersaulting

For more information and permission forms,
contact Parks Department

My mom's face got grim. (She was embarrassed.) She told the director it was truly misleading the way it was written on the poster, so the best thing to do now would be to add the somersault race. She said she knew one little boy, anyway, who would be very disappointed if they didn't. The director said it was too late to add anything, but maybe next year.

I just walked away. I looked back once, and my mother was still arguing . . . my mother and that director with the big white brand-new running shoes and the clipboard. And the mean back. She had a mean back, that director, and a mean haircut, too. I could tell that she would never change her mind for Petey. Never. I could tell she didn't like my mother explaining to her what to do, either.

I just kept going. I didn't even think out where I was going or what I was going to do or who was taking care of my scooter or how Nanette would feel . . . or about Petey. My legs just did the work of moving me away from there . . . away and up.

Each row of seats was a giant step. But my legs made that step and the next step and the step after that and the next. I stepped over lunches, baby things, even babies, dogs, hands. I heard someone say, "Hey, watch where you're putting that foot!"

I had to get away from that director, from the races,

124

from my mom, from my scooter, from Nanette, and—
most of all—from Petey (if he ever got there). What
could I tell him? There was not a single thing I
could bear to tell him!

I went right to the topmost step. I boosted myself up
into a little curved opening in the back wall. It just fit
me. I was looking down on the whole stadium and
up Melon Hill Avenue.

I saw Petey and Mrs. Greiner running down the hill.
What was that ridiculous Mrs. Greiner running for,
pulling Petey along with her, when there wasn't even
going to be a somersault race? And Petey's parents could
just as well take the whole day to get there, like I could
see they were going to, for all it mattered now. It
wouldn't even matter if they didn't get there at all!

What were they having a Field Day for, anyway? What
was the point of it? What?

I made up my mind I would just sit up there for the
whole Field Day. This Field Day was not _my_ Field Day,
anyway. It wasn't _my_ borough or _my_ city because we had
just moved here, anyway. And Nanette didn't live here,
either. The day right after Field Day she'd have to go
away again. So what did I care, anyway? I undid my
barrettes. My hair came unbraided. I took off my
sneakers. A man was making a speech. There was music.

125

I heard them announcing the first race and it sounded far, far away . . . <u>good</u> and far away.

I had an end of brown chalk in my shorts pocket. I wrote on the wall with it. When it was down to nothing, I wrote with the end of my finger in the chalk dust. I rubbed it right into the cement.

26

Going out to win...

Oh we're going out to win!

Suddenly my mother was in front of me. She could hardly catch her breath, but she pulled me right out of my place there in the wall. She jammed my sneakers back on and did them up tight. She pulled me down those bleacher steps . . . one step after the other without stopping.

"Jump," she ordered me.

"Don't treat me like a baby," I said.

"Don't act like a baby!" she yelled.

Everyone was listening. Everyone could hear. She said

127

I was a dumb kid. She said I didn't know as much as I
thought I knew. She said I <u>had</u> to be in the Field Day,
especially after I practically broke my head practicing on
that scooter. "You can't go through life sulking," she
said.

"I'm <u>not</u> sulking," I told her. And I said that I liked it
up there where you could see everything and that if Petey
couldn't be in <u>his</u> race I certainly wouldn't . . .

"No sacrifices, please," she said. It wouldn't help Petey
one bit! If I cared to get off my high horse and look, she
would show me Petey running along the bleachers and he
was just fine. She reminded me there was Nanette, who
was my guest, to think of, too.

She braided my hair and pinned it back up tight. I
screamed.

"That hurts!" I told her.

"Run!" she said. "Just shut up and run!" Just then
the woman with the megaphone called out, "Elana Rose
Rosen to the 514 Melon Hill Avenue relay team
immediately!"

Jimmy and Vinh and Nanette pushed me second in line.
It was my turn next, and I took off right across that relay
field. My shoe that my mom hadn't got quite back on over
my heel fell off. But with just one shoe I ran faster than I
ever ran in my whole life.

Every one of us from 514 ran faster than we ever ran anywhere before. We just went wild waiting till the one in front of us could touch us on our shoulder so we could take off again.

There were lots of other teams running the relay at the same time. All across the field, teams were running faster than they ever ran before, and even so their friends were yelling, "Faster! Faster! Faster!"

But the 514 Melon Hill Avenue relay team ran fastest of everybody. Then the head of the Parks Department announced the blue ribbon for our team for the very first race of the very first Field Day in borough history.

We all hugged each other. Petey ran to us and hugged me and Nanette. And I ran over to check that my scooter was safe with my mom. And to say hi. And to get a drink or something. Then I ran back to the track with Nanette to see what was happening next.

27

RUN

NEVER GOING TO STOP RUNNING?

Aɴᴅ ʀᴜɴ ɪs ᴡʜᴀᴛ we did all that day. No matter what else we did, what exact races we were in, in between we never stopped running.

We ran to my mom and Cecelia and Mrs. Greiner for watermelon and fruit punch. We ran to the drinking fountain and to the soda stand. We ran to the running track and the sand pits to watch the other kids. We had to run over and over to the platform to hear whose event it was next. We ran from one side of the bleachers to watch the band, especially to see the tuba player's cheeks get so fat we thought she'd burst. Then we ran right to the other side, where all the brand-new blue and red and white ribbons with gold writing were piled in their boxes. And in between we ran up the bleacher steps and down the bleacher steps and along the bleacher steps.

One of those times I ran by my mom and she grabbed me and held me by my shirt.

"Calm down!" she said. "Your face is bright red." She held out her little pocket mirror for me to look in.

"You gotta be careful. You can bust a blood vessel, honey, on a hot day like this," Mrs. Greiner said.

I held my hand out in front of my face. I could feel my face was hot . . . was burning. I liked my hot face. "I don't care," I told them.

"You just don't care about anything, do you?" my mom laughed. She held on to me close. I gave her a big kiss.

"Stay here a minute and cool off," she said.

I held out my T-shirt from my tummy so the breeze could come up under. I looked all around and counted flags, rust and gold for our borough, blue and orange for our city, on tall poles all the way around the stadium and those silver balloons strung in between and all the kids with their colored shirts running around.

The sun was hot and bright. I had to squint. And squinting made the colors run into each other so everything looked like a big, like a huge, a giant flower.

131

All of a sudden it came out of my own mouth to my mother and Mrs. Greiner that this was so far the best and most special and luckiest day ever in my whole life.

"You don't really mean your whole life?" my mom asked.

"In my whole life! I'm sure," I told her.

My mom looked at me and shook her head like she does.

"You are too much," she said. "First you go shrink yourself up in a crack in the wall, and you won't come down. And now it's the luckiest . . . and the most special . . . and the best."

"So what's wrong with that?" Mrs. Greiner said. "That just means it's a zigzag day."

My mother looked at Mrs. Greiner. She had never thought of such a thing. "A zigzag day?" she repeated.

Mrs. Greiner made swoops up and down with her hand in the air. "Mountains," she said. "And valleys. So. Zig . . . zag."

Mrs. Greiner might just be the smartest person in the whole Melon Hill project. Because zigzag turned out to be the perfect name for that day: how it began with our beautiful shirts and then with Petey's family being such a mess about getting ready. Then how it ended, which was in the newspapers and will go down in history, I'm sure.

132

But I'll show you, like Mrs. Greiner did with her hands. Only it's easier to show it on paper.*

As you see at zigs fifteen and sixteen, I did win the scooter race and the scooter event, and I did get the blue ribbons. I'm going to keep them right by my name on my screen around my bed. Whenever I look at those blue ribbons, I'll remember exactly how it was from the minute I first heard, "Elana Rose Rosen to the scooter race." How I was so scared, my T-shirt was stuck to me with sweating. But when they shouted, "<u>Go</u>!" I went. We all went. Except one kid who couldn't unstick his brake, which is exactly what I was afraid would happen to me.

When I came around and around again I could hear Nanette shouting. I could hear my mom. I heard Mrs. Greiner. And Jimmy Beck (yes!) and Adrienne and Siobhan and Beryl and Vinh and Cecelia. I saw Eduard stopped on his skateboard, watching. Coming around again, I saw Petey waving from Jimmy Beck's shoulders. (Of course, his parents never even got there.) "LANNY!" I heard. Everyone heard.

But you know, what I wanted to tell you is, I couldn't exactly hear or see any of this. It just <u>slid</u> by. And slid by

---

*See pages 136–137 for complete diagram of Zigzag Day (courtesy Mrs. Greiner).

133

again because the sweetest thing, the best thing in the whole world right then, was how the scooter and I traveled so fast and so smooth, around and around, taking the corners like . . . like fishes. Goldfish really swim corners like that.

It was magic. It was miraculous. It was the luck of Elana Rose Rosen. It was the opposite of what happened to poor Adrienne (zag eleven) in the double Dutch contest when the rope wouldn't turn fast and nothing went right even though any other time Adrienne is the best! I was sure . . . I <u>knew</u> I was riding that scooter the best I could.

And the reason it shows a double zig on the diagram is because after the scooter race went so fine the scooter tricks event came in fine, too. I did my double heel click and my triple. I've been a little afraid of that since the day I crashed and had to go to the hospital.

When I did that, Nanette hollered out, "Lanny! Scooter champion of the world!" My mom was embarrassed. She put her hand over Nanette's mouth. I wasn't embarrassed. I wanted her to shout it out to the whole world. I loved being champion.

But then there was a very deep zag. Zag twenty-one. (I've finally decided to call the low ones zags, because zag rhymes with sag while zig rhymes with big.)

That happened right after the wheelbarrow race. We were all walking to the stage to receive our ribbons. I had a bad feeling right in the back of my head. I whirled around fast, and there was Petey walking out to the running track all by himself.

Of course no one was there. Everyone was over at the stage. Petey stood looking all around. Then he started in to somersault. But he quit when he saw no one else was coming to join him. He tried one time again and stopped again.

I ran over to get him. I hated to tell him what had happened about the somersault race. I was so mad that not my mom and not Mrs. Greiner ever even told him there wasn't going to be any somersault race. And his parents never even got there, so they couldn't do anything. Everyone thought just because he didn't ask he didn't care . . . just because he was having fun it would be okay. They didn't know like I knew how much he practiced and how much he wanted to show everyone how terrific he was.

Now he wouldn't walk with me. When I tried to carry him over to the stage, he tore away and sat on the bleacher steps. He let his head go right down on his chest. (Petey's mother yells when he does that. She claims

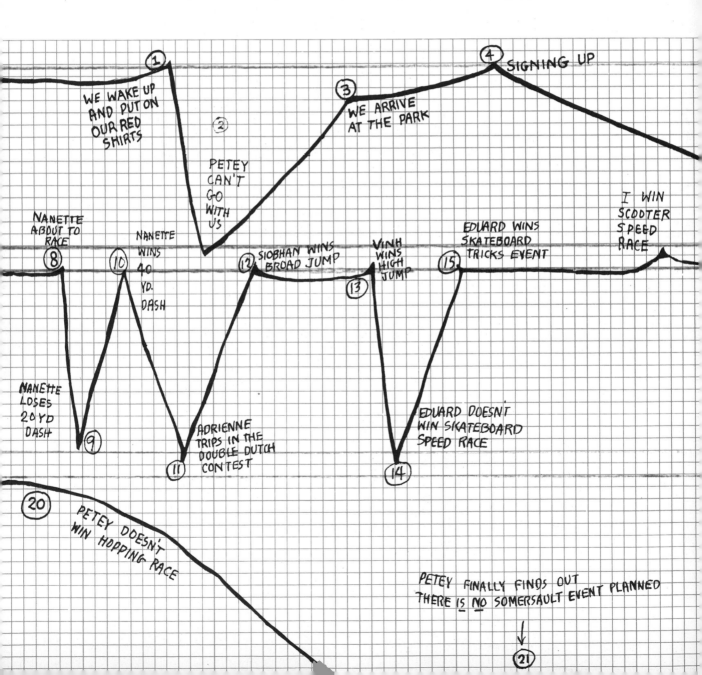

that's the reason Petey can't talk, because he squinches his voice box by hanging his head down.) But I left him there, anyway. I wanted to go get my blue ribbons from the mayor along with the other 514 kids.

Now we come to zig twenty-two. About that one . . . I just have to tell you in complete detail.

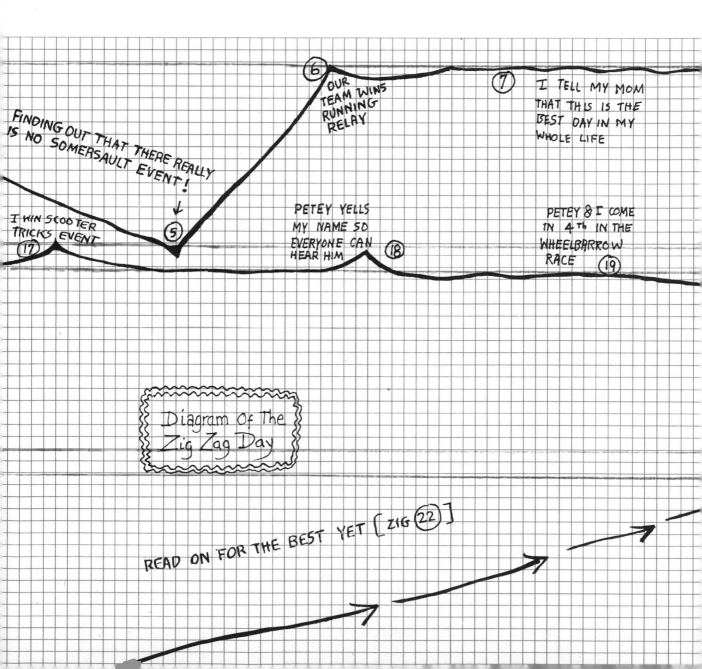

FINDING OUT THAT THERE REALLY IS NO SOMERSAULT EVENT!

6 OUR TEAM WINS RUNNING RELAY

7 I TELL MY MOM THAT THIS IS THE BEST DAY IN MY WHOLE LIFE

I WIN SCOOTER TRICKS EVENT

17

5

PETEY YELLS MY NAME SO EVERYONE CAN HEAR HIM

18

PETEY & I COME IN 4th IN THE WHEELBARROW RACE 19

Diagram Of The Zig Zag Day

READ ON FOR THE BEST YET [ZIG 22]

28

SUMMER IS ALMOST
OVER AND
MY WISH IS
EVERYBODY I LOVE SHOULD
REMEMBER
SOMETHING SO
AMAZING AND
UNUSUAL
LIKE THE EVENT
THAT HAPPENED NEXT

"CHILDREN, the games are over. Join your parents at the gates immediately," we heard the parks commissioner saying loud and clear over the loudspeakers. The word

138

immediately came out extra loud, so I jumped. I could
tell that parks commissioner was getting impatient.

But we still didn't move toward the gates. I was
standing with Nanette and Petey. We were on the edge
of the crowd on the side far from the gates. It's where
Gretel Green starts. That's the biggest lawn in the park.
It was where Petey had done his best and longest roll of
somersaults.

"Look!" Nanette said. "It's like there are hundreds of
statues."

It did look like hundreds of statues, because you could
see all our heads and shapes looking dark and the sky
looking light in the distance, which is how it gets at
sunset.

Then one of the statues started to move. It was Petey.
He put the top of his head down on the grass. He
joined his hands in front of his head and he flipped
right over.

I watched him do three somersaults. Then I put my
head down and flipped over. Nanette put her head down
and flipped over. Adrienne flipped over . . . Siobhan . . .
then Eduard . . . then everyone around me . . . then
everyone on Gretel Green as far as you could see.

Mrs. Greiner told us later (she loves telling this story)
it was the most amazing sight of her entire life and that

139

her Petey had started it. With his three perfect somersaults, the whole of Gretel Green was on the move, was moving. Every single kid was somersaulting like his life depended on it, and you couldn't see even a bit of grass.

"C'mon, you kids. Supper is waiting!" "Tomorrow is another day!" "If you don't come home this minute, there'll be no Field Day for you next year!" "Enough is enough." Parents called. They hollered. They threatened. And mostly we heard them okay. But we all just went right on somersaulting and rolling farther and farther away from them till we could hardly hear them at all.

Petey was way out in front of all the other kids. He was somersaulting down that hill where Gretel Green joins on to Long Lawn. But I was pretty close behind him, and I just knew I would never stop somersaulting till Petey stopped. So what did it really matter that everyone was yelling at us to stop and come home?

And I had grass in my mouth. My barrettes were lost. My hair was in my eyes. I felt like the elastic in my shorts had snapped. But I didn't stop somersaulting. I bumped into Eduard. We were going so fast now everyone was bumping. We laughed so much we had to sit up a minute. But it was just to get our breath, and we went right back into somersaulting.

The sky was turning pink. A huge moon was coming up, big and orange as the sun. Then the sky got dark. The trees got dark. The moon turned white like the regular moon. And we were all still somersaulting.

None of us stopped till Petey stopped. When Petey couldn't make another somersault I didn't make another and neither did Nanette. No one did. We just lay there catching our breath.

I was looking up at the moon. I thought how it would be to be the face in the moon looking down right then on Melon Valley Park. If I were that face in the moon I would be able to see kids from all over our borough, hundreds of kids spread out just whichever way we landed, lying there catching our breath, resting as though our parents were a million miles away. . . .

I reached over to Nanette and pulled her up. Nanette and I ran over and pulled Petey up. We swung him around and around. "Petey!" we yelled. "Petey gets the blue ribbon for somersaulting!" The kids from 514 ran over. Adrienne, Vinh, Jimmy, Eduard, Siobhan, and Beryl. They shouted, too. "Petey . . . Petey!" And the kids from 515, 516, 517, and 518, too. "Petey gets the blue ribbon for somersaulting."

Then our parents were there. A few were laughing, but most were mad. They were yelling in different languages.

Some people I saw whacked their kids and yanked them toward the gates. But Mrs. Greiner, of course, was just the opposite. She was yelling, "Bravo! Bravo, Petey!" like she was at an opera. As soon as she got through the crowd to Petey, she hoisted him off Jimmy Beck's shoulders onto her own. My mom yelled to her to watch out for her bad back (that she complains about), but she started right up Melon Hill with Petey on her shoulders. Nanette was carrying Mrs. Greiner's purse and shopping bags, so she ran after her. I started to follow, but my mom held me back.

My mom handed me my scooter. She didn't look too pleased with me, either.

"Elana, I'll just never understand you. We had a whole big ample Field Day. Right?" (I knew she didn't really want an answer.) "You won two blue ribbons. Right? Your friends won. I was clapping and rooting for you all the way, wasn't I? And so was Mrs. Greiner. And Cecelia . . . The whole borough, even! But that wasn't enough for you. You had to add a whole Field Day of your own on top of it. It's just never enough for you." She shook her head and had that expression meant to tell me I am a person beyond any normal mother's comprehension.

So of course I didn't try to explain how truly ultimately

necessary it was for me to follow Petey and how
somersaulting out on Gretel Green was enormously
a different thing than the real Field Day.

29

WHAT WILL YOU DO IN THE SOMEDAY TIME? HOW WILL YOUR DREAMS COME OUT?

I JUST FOLLOWED my mom out of the park to catch up with Nanette and Mrs. Greiner and Petey, and since we were the last to leave we heard the big gates clang closed behind us.

Then we had that long walk back up Melon Hill Avenue. Melon Hill seemed like a glass hill. I felt like I would slide right back down, I was suddenly so tired. Mrs. Greiner, who had let my mom take Petey down from her shoulders, slipped behind me and Nanette. We felt her hands against our backs helping push us along home. She was the only one of us still talking.

144

"You'll see," she said to my mother. "Next year they'll have to put that somersault race right in the program. If I was the mayor I'd put it at the end . . . like the kids did it tonight. After they give out the ribbons and play music, before we all go home. I love a party."

"Yeah," my mother said.

"And another thing . . ." Mrs. Greiner went on.

"What?" my mother said. I could tell she was just getting more and more irritated.

"Next year Petey will be able to enter in all the regular races. Next year when Nanette comes for Field Day"— Nanette and I grabbed hands, thrilled that someone else knew she and I would be together for Field Day always!— "Petey could be winning races, maybe even talking. But talk or not, he'll be right in there with all the other kids. Won't you, little champ?" she said.

Petey was holding my mom's hand, but he twisted around to smile at Mrs. Greiner.

"I wouldn't make predictions, Rachel," my mom said, and walked on ahead, pulling Petey along. She sounded tired, and she had those tired shoulders though she walked very fast like she always does.

I got on my scooter and caught up alongside her and Petey. "Did you call for a taxi, lady?" I asked. She gave me a little whack on the behind with her purse, laughing.

145

"Take Nanette and Petey in your cab," she said. "I want to walk with Rachel."

Nanette and Petey got on in back. We squashed together and rode through the courtyard and right up to the door of 514. Mr. Portelli was there, looking at Jimmy and Siobhan's blue ribbons. He opened the door wide for us so we could ride up to the elevator door (even though you're not supposed to). And the elevator door opened so we could ride right on in.

Nanette said wouldn't it be great if we could ride right up to 8E, and my door would swing open for us and we could coast right in. . . .

"And then," I said, "we could coast on into the bathroom and over the edge of the tub and splash into our bath."

"And then," Nanette said, "we'd coast out of the tub and into bed, and in the morning when I have to go home we could just take the scooter again and ride right out your window and the scooter would be able to fly. . . ."

"And you and me would be pilots and Petey would be the navigator, and we'd scooter-fly to your house in Toronto. . . ."

"Only first, we'd go somewhere else on the way just to see," Nanette said.

"And maybe somewhere else after that place," I said.

"And no one in the whole wide . . . ," Nanette started to recite in a singsong. Then we recited Grandma's prediction together. "And no one in the whole wide world will ever be able to tell all the wonderful places we will go and all the wonderful things we will do. . . ."

Of course we missed our elevator stop and went on to the ninth floor and then all the way back down to the lobby, where my mom and Mrs. Greiner got in, and all five of us together rode back up to eight.

So this is the last thing I have to tell you. It's neither a zig nor a zag. It's just

THE END

EXCEPT

THIS IS HOW MUCH OLDER I AM THAN
WHEN I FIRST MOVED TO MELON HILL!

2 MONTHS +1 WEEK OR

9 WEEKS + 6 DAYS OR

69 DAYS OR

1,656 HOURS OR

99,360 MINUTES OR

5,961,600 SECONDS !